Carbon

Katie Davis

DEDICATION

Thank you to my loving friends and family that helped me make this book a reality. I couldn't have done this without your help and support.

A special thanks to Hillary Leung for working on content editing with me during the early stages of this book.

CONTENTS

CHAPTER 1

The sun glimmered on the edge of the horizon, casting a warm orange glow over the huts. A cold sea wind swirled amongst the tattered canvas rooftops, causing them to flutter.

It was still too early for most of the refugees to be awake. They remained curled up in their huts, trying to stay warm. The only person outside was a teenage girl that darted from raft to raft, making her way towards land.

Emma squeezed between the huts, pressing herself through the narrow passageways. She was a scrawny, black-haired girl with lanky limbs and looked like she had missed more meals than not.

She picked up speed when the space between the huts was wide enough. She wanted to be in and out of the market as soon as possible today. She knew the longer it took, the more likely it was she'd be caught. Getting caught was never in the best interests of a refugee, especially one like her.

Emma slowed as she approached the city limits, catching her breath. The sea air sunk heavily in her lungs. Running had made her chest ache. So she waited a few moments and let the view of the city sink in.

The dark grey, seemingly endless wall stretched out for miles along the shoreline in front of her. It had been built to separate Campton's citizens from the refugees, and she was on the wrong side. Only two gates passed in and out of the city, and both were well guarded.

Emma needed to get into the heart of the city, something that was rarely done by other refugees.

She stood at a small clearing between the huts. The cold wind blew hard at her as she watched the top of the wall. The guards switched positions, facing their backs towards her.

Now.

Her feet leapt out from under her. She sprinted towards the drainage pipe.

Her heart pounded in her chest as she darted to the opening. Luckily, the guards hadn't spotted her.

The large metal pipe opened out of the wall, spitting sewage and waste into a stream that led to the sea. Emma repressed the urge to vomit as she pulled a dingy handkerchief from her pocket and tied it around her face.

She let out a long, slow breath and concentrated on the rush of sewage. Every day refugees splashed through this to get into the city for work and food. They often fell deathly ill later. It was hard to keep clean in these conditions, and open wounds or illness was often a death sentence.

Emma had been born an elementalist, and that kept her alive.

An intense heat surged through her body.

She sensed the chemical structure of the water moving and shifting around her. It became an extension of her hands, and fell under her control. Her slender hands pushed forward in one swift motion and forced the water to flow up against gravity and make a path for her into the city.

Emma closed her eyes against the bright lights as she stepped out of the sewers into the city. Sunlight reflected off the metal rooftops and scattered small sparkles of light throughout the street. Stained glass windows played with the light and cast brilliant reds, blues, and greens across the whitewashed houses. The city was vibrant, and even with most citizens still tucked away in their beds, it felt alive.

It was a different world beyond the wall – a better one. It was a world Emma wished she could share with her brother, Zak, but the citizens of Campton despised the refugees.

The residents in the outer circle worked on the fishing boats like her, the only difference was they had these homes to go to after a long day of gutting fish. They were born in this country, not forced here as refugees of war, so they were allowed in the city. Unlike Emma and Zak, they had real homes, not a thrown together shack on the water.

Emma turned away from the row of houses, cutting her day dreams short. She had to focus. It was crucial that she get into position before the market opened.

City guards paced the streets, watching for any signs of trouble. Their suits of armor creaked as they marched, and their swords glinted as they swung in their sheaths.

Emma felt safer now that she was on the inside of the wall, but she was careful not to make eye contact with any of the guards. Refugees weren't allowed in the city, especially during the King's Market.

Normally her appearance would have given her away, but today her long black hair was neatly combed and she had splurged on a bright pink lipstick. She looked at her reflection in a nearby window and decided it would have to do.

The streets of the inner city bustled with activity as shopkeepers adjusted their signs and swept their porches. Cart owners set up their wares in courtyards, and merchants laid out every kind of merchandise imaginable. One shop was setting out rich colorful silks; another hung pelts and fur coats. But the one that caught Emma's eye was a cart with gold and silver pendants hanging neatly around it. She was careful not to let her gaze linger, in case she was being watched.

Citizens critiqued the goods loudly, their heavy purses jingling as they walked. An old man's laugh echoed above the chatter. Emma smelled stale tobacco and whiskey as he walked past her towards a spice merchant with a long, twisty black beard.

Emma watched as the men exchanged jokes and bartered. For them, this was just another chance to dress up and show off. It was a foreign concept to her.

Thousands of people were flocking into the city today, dressed in their finest silks and jewels. Ladies wore their hair stacked high, with single curls draping down their powder covered faces. Men sucked on pipes and twirled their curly beards and moustaches.

The guards would be busy watching the gates into the city today, trying to keep the refugees out. The temptation of a rich woman's necklace was more than most could resist. Who could blame them when it could feed their children for months?

Emma doubted more than a dozen would-be thieves would make it in besides herself. Most would never pass the gates.

No one appeared to be watching her now, so she decided it was safe to put her plan into action.

"One cinnamon bun, please," she said to a gray-haired woman behind the table of fresh pastries.

Emma held out a single copper coin and smiled.

The woman took the coin and handed her a bun in an almost mechanical fashion; she did not return eye contact. Emma wasn't surprised. Despite looking neater than usual, she was still plain compared to most citizens. She wore plain cotton pants and an old leather jacket, not silk or fur like most of the women.

This cinnamon bun was a rare treat, but she felt guilty at the cost. She had only bought the bun to help legitimize her disguise. The people around her could have one whenever they pleased, it made her more jealous than she cared to admit. For her a normal day meant stale bread crusts, discarded pieces of fish, and the odd moldy bit of cheese.

Walking slightly faster than the crowd, Emma hurried down the lane of merchants. There were all kinds of people around her - guards, merchants, court members, and dignitaries.

"Eww, a filthy little girl just touched me," a woman said as Emma passed her.

Embarrassed, Emma picked up the pace and kept her head down.

Relax. You haven't done anything wrong yet.

She stopped once she reached the Royal Square. It was the exact center of the city, and the heart of the King's Market. It was breathtaking. Glass shimmered in the light of the morning sun, and the cobblestone streets looked like they were made of gold. Emma found herself daydreaming again about what it would be like to live in a house here with a crackling fireplace that she could read by. It was nothing like the dreary world Emma usually lived in. She breathed it all in, before forcing herself to focus again.

Guards were everywhere. They watched intently as the merchants laid out their wares. Their eyes darted amongst the crowd, like hawks watching a field of mice, waiting to strike. Emma would only have one chance, and she couldn't afford to blow it. She looked at the silver cart from earlier. It gleamed brightly, bouncing spots of light on the cart with multi-colored silk thread next to it.

Emma was relieved – her story would be believable. She had gotten lucky this year. If anyone asked, she was the daughter of a seamstress and at the market to buy silk thread. She hoped it would be enough to explain why she was there.

With her anxiety lessened, she decided to sit on the warm, dry grass nearby and eat her cinnamon bun. She positioned herself so the guards could see her, and hoped it would reduce any suspicion they might have.

Her mouth watered as the golden syrup ran down her boney fingers. This was the first time she'd eaten a pastry in years. The smell of cinnamon lingered in the air as she gobbled down the last few bites. She reminded herself to buy one for Zak later.

A gong rang out loudly to signal the start of the market. Emma turned her head towards the sound, craning her neck to get a better view of the commotion.

A deafening roar of voices grew through the crowd as people began a fierce wave of bartering and cheering. People traditionally haggled at the beginning of the market. If they didn't like the prices, they'd drink their whiskey and beer before coming back to try a bit harder. It seemed like a crude habit to Emma, but tradition was important in Campton. At the very least, the guards were distracted.

Emma stood up and walked straight towards her target. Her eyes flicked over to the silver cart. There were a few pieces lying haphazardly on the edge of the table, just out of the merchant's direct view. Those were her target.

She snatched the silver bars and tucked them into her pack as soon as the merchant was distracted by another customer. Emma felt a sudden surge of relief as she twisted her body back towards the silk merchant. Now she just had to sell that she was here as a patron, and pray no one had seen her make the grab.

"How much for the purple thread?" Emma asked, trying to feign as much interest as possible. She stood up straight and looked the lanky old man in the eye, hoping to hide her nervousness.

"Ten silver," he said. "I won't take any less than that, and I know you don't have enough."

He turned away to face another customer.

Emma slammed a hand on the table and said, "It's barely worth seven."

The shopkeeper glared at her. His eyes reminded her of a rat, beady and cold.

"I'll give it to you for eight, and that's final."

"It isn't worth that!"

"Then you aren't buying from me," he said.

His attention turned away from Emma again, making it clear he was no longer interested in her. She feigned dejection and walked away from the cart toward the outer edge of the square with her shoulders slumped.

The other shopkeeper would notice the missing silver soon. She needed to get far enough away that the guards wouldn't catch her.

Suddenly, Emma felt a hand clamp down hard on her shoulder. She jumped and turned around.

The rugged face of a guard stared down at her.

"Think you've got a clever trick, don't you?" He smirked at her, and raised a bushy eyebrow. "Talk to one merchant while you scam off the other. Not a bad plan. Might have worked too, but I caught the shine from the silver going into that pack o' yours."

Emma's heart pounded in her throat.

Her vision narrowed and her eyes glazed over. She couldn't breathe, it felt like a clamp was pressing in on her lungs. How far could she get get if she ran? Her back blazed with pain as she remembered being caught two years ago.

Not again.

She flinched.

"Don't think of running, girl. It's to the guardhouse now. That much silver must be worth a death sentence under the King's new laws."

Emma glared at the unflinching face of the guard. He had to be bluffing; she'd have heard of the new laws, especially if it was as extreme as a death sentence. Wouldn't she? Sweat dribbled down her back, and her mouth grew dry. Her body shivered with the sudden realization of what was at stake. She had made a grave mistake.

Run. Just run!

#

Emma wouldn't stop; she had to keep running.

The guards closed in on her as she bolted through the crowded streets. Whistles blew and shouts of "catch her!" followed from behind.

She pushed the air around her, creating a pulse that shoved a fat, burly man in a thick wool jacket out of her way. She hated using her abilities in public, but now she had no choice.

The way out of the city seemed longer now that every turn and alleyway was critical to her escape. Houses and shops muddled together in a passing blur of colors. She needed to lose the guards that were chasing her without getting lost or cornered.

She turned down a narrow alley and lost a larger guard, but another one caught up to her shortly after she emerged on the other end. There were too many in the city today; the only solution was to make it to the sea. She could outrun them there and hide in the rafts.

"Stop!" a guard yelled from a few hundred feet behind her.

He was winded.

Good.

"There's no use running."

Emma shrieked and tumbled to the ground. It felt like a knife had shot through her shoulder; hot sticky blood poured down her arm. The guard had struck her from behind with a piece of iron. It lodged deep in her shoulder.

Emma closed her eyes as the pain throbbed throughout her body. She took a deep breath and regained her footing before taking off again.

She could see the wall. Soon she'd be at the sewage pipes.

I might make it!

Surging forward, she ran at full speed towards the wall.

Another shot ripped through her leg. Emma crumbled to the ground, her face grinding into the cobblestone road. Her jawbone cracked loudly on impact. Blood ran down her neck, staining the grey streets a rusty red.

She pushed herself up on her uninjured arm. She wavered and struggled to support herself. She was too weak to hold herself up.

She toppled back to the ground.

"Stupid bitch," the guard said as he grabbed Emma by the hair and lifted her up. "I told you there was no point running."

The other guards jogged towards them. Emma wanted to run, but she wasn't able to break free. Everything felt blurry and dull as she blinked away tears. She had never felt such intense pain.

The guard ignored her cries of pain and the pool of blood that had formed at her feet. He tossed Emma over his shoulder and said, "I'll make sure they execute you for this."

Her entire body was on fire as a tremendous flood of strength surged over her. She'd never felt this much desperation. Her heart raced, pounding in her ears.

He's going to kill me.

Emma's body took over, and a force she didn't know she was capable of pushed itself out of her and into the guard. She wasn't sure what she was doing, but somehow she knew it would stop him.

The guard's body became rigid, his arms froze in mid-air, his legs twisted. His knees trembled and gave out under him as they both crashed to the ground.

Emma turned her head to look at the guard beside her. His face was a pasty white, and as he opened his mouth, blood poured down his stubbled chin. His eyes were fixed on Emma as he took his final breath.

CHAPTER 2

Charles Cavallaro was a tall, muscular man. His white beard was thick, but neatly trimmed to about an inch in length. He kept his hair cropped short, and wore a dark blue and gold navy uniform.

He had been called for unexpected, urgent business in Campton. A young refugee had caused a stir amongst the local guards, and his attention as Captain was required. The guardhouse was abuzz with rumors and speculations about the girl sleeping in front of him.

She was a small thing, frail and underfed. Her ribs protruded visibly as she breathed with a sickly sharpness. Charles watched her curiously. He had expected something more exciting when he got an emergency message. He was a little disappointed. This girl, despite the rumors, didn't seem to be as impressive as he'd hoped.

"Sir," a voice said, breaking the silence of the room.

It was a young cadet that looked barely twelve. He was lanky and awkward. He fidgeted with his hands as he spoke.

"The nurse says she may be able to wake her with some smelling salts - if you approve, that is."

Charles stroked his beard and nodded. The sooner this girl woke up, the sooner he could learn if she'd been worth his time. Besides, it had taken him all day to get here and she hadn't stirred yet.

Once the girl was awake he'd know if the men were mistaken about her ability to work carbon. It hadn't been heard of in years, let alone from a child. That combined with the power to kill a full-grown man was unheard of, even before the war. He assumed the men had exaggerated their report.

A short woman in a white dress walked in clutching a small snuff bottle. She edged carefully around the captain towards the sleeping girl. Her fingers quivered as she held the bottle under the girl's nose and waited. The nurse held her breath and a trickle of sweat dripped down her forehead.

The girl began to cough and her eyes fluttered. She thrust her head to the side and continued coughing while the nurse ran out of the room.

Charles leaned closer, resting his elbows against his legs.

The girl lightly pulled against the shackles that held her to the bed. Her eyes blinked open.

Realizing that she was restrained, she struggled against the shackles and screamed.

She looked at Charles with wide, hazel eyes, then back to the shackles on her wrists. A wave of heat passed over Charles as the girl broke the steel shackles like they were made of paper.

He smiled.

"So, they were right about you," he said. "At least the part about working carbon. I'm Captain Cavallaro. You may call me Charles. Who are you?"

The girl froze and stared at him. She bit at her lower lip and trembled, dropping her gaze to the ground.

"Emma." She stuttered. "P-p-please don't kill me. Please."

Charles laughed.

"I didn't spend all day on a boat to come and kill you."

Charles chuckled softly and motioned to the young cadet that stood near the door.

"You must be starving. Bring Emma a bowl of soup."

The cadet jolted to attention and briskly left. Charles knew this girl was a potential threat, but something made him feel at ease looking at her. She seemed more scared than dangerous.

"What happened?" Emma fiddled with her blanket and avoided eye contact. She scanned the plain wood-panelled room of the guardhouse.

"You don't remember the King's Market?" Charles leaned back in his chair and crossed his legs. "I heard it was quite the spectacle. People came from all over to attend. You even managed to take a souvenir from a certain silver merchant. Do you remember that?"

Emma looked up at him, holding her breath. The events of the afternoon were apparently coming back to her.

"Okay, so you remember that at least. How about when the guard chased you, do you remember what happened after that?"

He grabbed the bowl of soup from the cadet that had just entered and passed it to Emma.

Emma looked down at the soup and set the spoon hastily on the bed beside her. She quickly began to slurp it down, ignoring the spoon.

Poor thing must have been starving.

"I'll remind you while you eat," he said. "You were being chased and got captured. You must have panicked and used your carbon working abilities to kill the guard."

He paused to watch Emma's reaction.

She stopped eating and looked up at him.

"That is almost impossible, since the Emperor of Ban Lian wiped out all the carbon elementalists to end the war. It is possible your family managed to survive and that is how you came to Campton as a refugee. But, that still leaves the problem of human chemistry. Being able to work carbon isn't enough. You'd have to know carbon, oxygen, hydrogen, nitrogen, calcium, phosphorous, and more to kill someone."

"I don't know what you mean," Emma said. She set the empty bowl next to her.

"With which part?"

"I don't know what those words mean."

"You don't know the names of elements?"

Emma shook her head. "I know some. Like silver, but none of those other things you said. I think you have me confused with someone else."

"No, no. Only someone with the ability to manipulate both carbon and iron could have broken those shackles."

Emma began to fidget.

Charles frowned and pointed to the door.

"I won't stop you if you run. But the guards might now that they know your secret, some of them are quite terrified of you."

Emma nodded, but said nothing.

"Now, back to your unique abilities." Charles leaned back in his chair and pulled a cigarette out of his jacket pocket. He put it to his lips and lit it. "You have an interesting ability to work elements without training. You don't know the chemical makeup of complex structures, but you are able to manipulate them anyways. This is quite rare."

He took a slow drag on his cigarette.

"With proper training you could be one of the strongest elementalists in the world. You'd be strong, rich, and respected by anyone you encountered. How does that sound? No more starving, no more hiding."

"I can't." Emma said quietly. "My brother needs me."

Charles took another drag on the cigarette and pondered what to say next. Getting this girl to come with was critical, he couldn't let her wander the streets. She was a definite threat if her powers were used the wrong way.

"I'll tell ya what. If you come with me, I'll make sure he gets everything he needs to live a long, happy life. Money, food, whatever he needs, and lots of it. We'll keep an eye on him as long as you work for us, and we'll make sure he's safe. Don't you want that life for him? "

Emma fell silent for a while.

"Of course I want that for him," she said. "But he'll be alone. I'd be abandoning him. "

Tears crept to the corners of her eyes. She blinked them away and sniffled.

"I'm sure you've dreamt of giving him a house to live in and enough food to eat. Be honest with yourself – he'll never have that if you stay here. Even if you can steal a chunk of silver each year, it'll never come close to what I'm offering you. "

Her eyes focused on the knotted wooden floor.

"I'll let you think about it overnight," Charles said after several minutes of silence. "We leave for Portishead tomorrow afternoon. I'll need your answer before then."

Emma tossed and turned for hours. She kept tossing Charles' offer around in her mind, listing out the pros and cons of her options. Zak would be sleeping alone in their ratty tent under the ripped and discolored canvas right now. The food she'd left him would be running out soon. She worried that he'd go out to look for her.

What if he slips into the sea?

The waters were unforgiving this time of year, the waves rough and icy. A slight misstep would suck him down and swallow him under the floating city of rafts. If he didn't drown, he'd freeze to death in minutes.

Emma sat up.

She couldn't stand it – she needed to see him, tell him what was going on and that she was okay. She leaned down and pulled on her tattered boots, quickly lacing them up her ankles. If she could find Charles, she would go with him, for a price. Zak would understand. She was obviously worth something to the King. If she could give Zak a life worth living, she'd give up hers doing whatever they asked.

A twinge of anticipation coursed through her, sending a shiver up her spine. She'd never felt like she had power, but now she knew the cards were in her hands. She could finally change her brother's fate.

Emma stuck her head out of the room into a narrow stone hallway. It was dark and smelled of damp, rich earth. She sucked in the air, savoring it as she walked down the hallway. It felt eerily quiet, the only noise was the soft padding of her footsteps.

There was a soft crunching noise behind her. Emma jumped and pushed her back up against the wall.

A pale hand came at her through the darkness, grabbing the collar of her shirt and lifting her off the ground. Screaming, Emma flung herself about trying to break free. Another hand quickly covered her mouth and nose. Her body froze with terror. She couldn't breathe.

"What are you doing out in the halls?" a deep voice demanded. "I told the Captain you were trouble, but he has a soft spot for little things like you."

Emma struggled against his grasp, pushing the air around her in a panic. He laughed at her and set her down.

"Everyone thinks you're so powerful," he mocked. "You're just a weak little girl with a couple tricks."

He leaned back on his rear leg and pushed his arms in a circular motion around his torso. A loud cracking noise pierced the room as several pieces of rock dislodged from the wall. The shards of rock hung menacingly in the air, waiting for him to strike.

Emma dodged the first few pieces that he hurled at her. She shifted left, right and left again but a small shard managed to clip her arm and pain shot through her shoulder. Her arm went numb down to her fingertips. She winced. As she tried to lift up her arm, she realized that it wouldn't budge.

"Pressure points are a wonderful thing," he said, his eyes fixated on her like she was prey. "I'll show you what someone with training can do, you little shit."

Emma had never met another elementalist, she didn't know what to do. This guard had paralyzed her right arm with a small, fragmented stone.

How is this even possible?

Her heart raced as she began to panic.

She pushed forward with her other hand, casting a thick wall of dirt towards the guard. As soon as it hit him, she bolted down the hall, hoping she had given herself enough time to get away and find Charles.

"I'll kill you!" he yelled as he pushed the dirt away from his eyes and chased after her. He gained ground quickly.

Emma swiftly turned the corners in the twisting hallways, dodging the stray stones that flew after her.

"Enough!"

A wall of stone erected itself in front of Emma. The guard had moved the entire wall to block her path. She didn't notice it in time to stop and ran full speed into the wall.

THUMP.

Emma's vision went dark and everything felt cold. She fell limply to her knees and her head cracked against the ground.

\#

"What the hell did you do that for? I could have you court marshaled for this!"

Charles was livid. His whole body felt warm as he screamed at the cadet. A vein pulsed in his neck.

"I gave direct orders that she was not to be harmed!"

"But, sir! She was out in the hall by herself --"

"My orders are not open for debate!" Charles shouted as he stared at the cadet. "You will follow them or you will leave immediately. Understood?"

"Yes, sir."

"Good, now get outta here before I change my mind."

Emma shifted on the bed, her finger reached to her temple where she'd been struck. It was covered in a thick white bandage with a small spattering of blood. Charles had found her within moments of the incident after being awoken by the commotion outside his room. He'd brought her back here and wrapped her head.

"Are you okay?" Charles leaned over her. "You need to stop getting head injuries."

"No kidding," Emma said softly.

"Well, anyways," he said. "At least there shouldn't be any permanent damage..."

Emma interrupted him, "I'll go with you."

Charles raised his eyebrow and looked at her, surprised.

"I'd like to accept. It's what's best for Zak," Emma said. Her voice shook.

Charles wondered if she really meant what she was saying. This was a lot to ask from a girl who was barely a teenager.

"That's great. We're excited to have you on board with us –"

"But you have to let me see him first, to check that he's okay and say goodbye," she said. Her voice was laced with urgency. She stumbled over her words as they flew out of her mouth. "Knowing him, he'll be worried sick. Please, let me see him before we go."

"I'm not unreasonable, Emma. I know how much your brother means to you, and of course I'll let you say goodbye. I'm sure he misses you."

The corner of her mouth raised to a hint of a smile.

"Emma, I really am quite glad that you'll be joining us."

She nodded and fiddled with her hands anxiously.

"We'll give you one thousand gold pieces to give to Zak," Charles said. "We're on a tight schedule though, so we have to leave this afternoon."

Emma nodded.

#

Emma stood on the raft she and Zak had painstakingly built. It was dingy and in desperate need of repair. The logs drifted apart as the rope stretched with each passing wave. She wondered how many times small things had been lost between the cracks and swallowed up by the cold, dark water. Probably more than she could count.

This place was all they had had for the last two years. Ever since they could remember, it was the only thing that had really been theirs.

Their tent was made of tattered canvas, hung up between three support beams that formed a triangle. They were both young when they made it, so they didn't have the skills for much else. It wasn't much, but it kept them safe enough from the wind and water. Emma had talked about building something better after the King's Market, but now she had other plans. Charles was waiting for her.

Emma cheered up a little as she thought about how much Zak's life was going to improve. Her fingers coursed over the canvas as she imagined a house with a fireplace that would keep him warm and comfortable. He'd be happy and safe, even without her here.

It was going to be hard, but saying goodbye had to be done. She ran through it in her mind: she would pull back the canvas, hug her brother, and explain to him what was going to happen. He'd cry, she'd cry, and they'd hug one last time before she handed him the bag of gold and left. Tears snuck to her eyes and her chest felt heavy.

It's time. Better to just get it over with.

Her fingers wrapped around the canvas and pulled a small section back. She stepped into the familiar tent, letting the musty smell wash over her before she opened her eyes.

Zak was gone.

Emma panicked, looking around the tent for any clues. She noticed a note pinned carefully to her small, tattered pillow.

I went into town to look for you. I'll be back at sunset. Hope you come home soon. Love, Zak.

Tears spilled from her eyes and streamed down her cheeks as she read the note over and over again. He wouldn't be back in time to say goodbye. She couldn't believe she wouldn't have the chance to hug him and tell him that she loved him before she left.

Maybe Charles would understand, and would let them stay for one more night – but no, it was time to go. She knew that.

She sucked in huge gulps of air, trying to stop sobbing as she thought about leaving him alone again.

She felt empty as she grabbed a pencil and a scrap of paper off the floor.

Zak,

I got caught stealing and was taken to the guardhouse. They told me I have to go with them to Portishead to join the Royal Guard, but they gave me this gold for you. You can finally get that dog you've always wanted, and a nice house! I love you more than anything, and I'm so sorry I couldn't see you to say goodbye. Please forgive me.

Love always, Emma.

By the time she was done writing, the paper was damp with tears. She carefully pinned it to the bag of gold she was leaving behind. She knew no one would come onto their raft except Zak. Everyone around them knew they never had anything worth stealing. No one really did out here.

He'd come home and find the gold with her note. He'd feel abandoned again, and maybe resent her, but it was the only way to give him a decent future.

She grabbed the note he left her and folded it before tucking it carefully into her pocket. It was all she'd have to remember him by in the capital.

Emma stepped into the cold sea wind one last time, and took a final look at her home. Her teeth chattered as the frigid air brushed against her tear soaked cheeks.

She trudged back along the rafts towards the shore, hoping against all hope that Zak would come running towards her before she left.

She knew she'd probably never return here, and part of her knew she might never see Zak again. But, for the first time in years, he would be safe, and that was all that mattered. Maybe – just maybe – he'd forgive her someday.

CHAPTER 3

Emma looked ahead nervously, steadying herself as the boat rocked from side to side. The waves echoed in her ears and caused her head to ache. She sank her body deeper into the seat.

Her stomach lurched and she felt bile in her mouth as the boat surged to the side. Her throat burned, making her cringe as she spat over the side of the railing. She was desperate for water, but wouldn't bring herself to ask any of the sailors. None had been hostile to her, but she felt out of place here. She'd rather suffer silently than introduce herself.

"How ya holdin up?" Charles came back to the upper deck just in time, carrying a tray of food and water.

Emma's heart leapt as she stared at the cup with drops of water condensing on the side.

"Seasick? Have some bread, it'll help."

She took it from him, trembling from the cold wind, and gobbled it down.

"Are you feeling better?" Charles asked as she drained the final sips of her glass.

Emma nodded. She still felt dizzy, but at least her stomach was calmer now.

"Have you ever been on a boat before?"

Emma nodded. She had been on fishing boats, but nothing that went this far out to sea.

"I still get seasick every now and then," Charles said. "On my first trip to Ban Lian, I was sick the whole way there and back! I've never felt worse. I thought I was going to die."

Charles talked about the voyage while Emma tried to pay attention. He carried on about the history of the navy, Captains and Admirals that he knew and worked with. He told her about the boat he was on, a small warship. She laughed whenever he did and nodded occasionally, but her eyes were focused on the shore.

They were at least a mile from land, but Emma could still see the rafts that lined up along the coast. Miles of rafts surrounded every city they passed. She couldn't believe that so many refugees lived on them. She had thought that her city was unique, that Campton was the only place that pushed refugees out into the sea on shaky makeshift homes. That couldn't have been further from the truth.

Her heart sank as she fixed her eyes on the rafts. Millions of people with nothing more than a couple of planks to call home lined the coast.

How many are there?

Emma was deep in thought, taking in the sights around her.

A bell rang, and immediately everyone hurried to the front of the ship. Some pulled ropes and grabbed at pulleys. Others rushed to the railings and cranked large steel wheels that made a screeching, wailing noise.

Emma pressed her hands to her ears, trying to block out the sound. The noise resonated through her bones as the bell kept ringing.

She cringed, trying to clasp her hands tighter over her ears.

How do they tune this out?

She watched them as they prepared the boat to dock.

"Are you okay, Emma?" Charles yelled over the bell.

"Yes, sir. It's just loud," Emma shouted back, hoping he could hear her.

Charles smiled and nodded.

Towards the front of the boat were two tall cliffs that towered on either side of them. They were passing through a canal that was barely wide enough for the boat. The cliff walls were made of sharp, jagged rocks that stretched hundreds of yards into the sky.

The boat passed within inches of the rocks as it continued into the canal. Emma was sure they'd crash at any moment. Her heart thumped loudly in her chest. She held her breath and shut her eyes anxiously. The worst-case scenario played on repeat in her mind.

Charles stood up and tapped Emma, startling her. He motioned for her to follow him to the edge, gesturing with his outstretched hand at the rocks. She hesitated, wanting to stay as far from the jagged rocks as possible.

"It's okay," Charles said with a reassuring smile. "Nothing will happen. Come and watch how we're avoiding the cliff."

Emma wasn't convinced, but she got up and trailed behind Charles. The sailors around her were focused intently on the walls. Their brows furrowed in concentration and their hands rested on the edge of the ship. Her heart raced as she approached the edge.

An intense heat radiated from them and moved downwards.

She opened her mouth to ask Charles about it, but he stretched out his hand to pull her forward so she could see over the railing.

Emma cautiously peeked over the edge. The rock wall was just inches in front of her as she leaned forward. She imagined that she could touch it with the tip of her nose if she stood on her tip toes. Warm steam rushed up over her face and coated her nostrils with the smell of salt.

The sailors worked the water around the boat, creating a cushion between the hull and the rocks. They were using their abilities to move the boat through the canal safely.

Suddenly, it all made sense – the heat, the intense concentration the sailors had. They were able to navigate safely between the rocky cliffs by moving the water.

"How are they doing that?" Emma said as she stared in amazement. She'd never heard of elementalists working together like this.

"They were all trained at the naval academy." Charles laughed, amused by how astounded she was. "It's rather amazing what a team of elementalists can do. You should see the mountain armies. The soldiers can move chunks of earth like they're nothing. They can clear a road through the mountains in only a few days."

Emma felt a little calmer. Something about knowing there were so many other elementalists out there made her feel less scared. While she was still unique because of her ability to work carbon, she wasn't completely alone. These sailors had a mastery of water. Charles told her that water was made of hydrogen and oxygen, and to move water you had to be able to work both of these. Emma wondered how she would ever keep all of this information straight.

"Emma?" Charles fixed his eyes squarely on hers. "How much do you know about the war?"

Emma shrugged and said, "Not much, just that a lot of people died."

She tried to tune out the conversation whenever people talked about it. She had always thought it was too depressing to think about since it couldn't be changed anyways.

Charles looked out over the water pensively and paused before continuing.

"King Terril and Emperor Chao were both new to the throne when the war started. They started a 5 year war that cost millions of lives after King Terril's young Queen was murdered. We're still not even sure who did it."

Charles shook his head and pinched the bridge of his nose with his thumb and index finger and sighed.

"The war was brutal in the early months. King Terril drafted huge armies of elementalists. The countryside was ravaged and burned, whole cities fell, and Emperor Chao responded by pulling all of his forces into Ban Lian to defend it."

"Is that when they built the wall?"

Charles nodded.

"They built the wall around the capital province, 500 square miles and hundreds of feet high. It was made of steel to protect the province of Ban Lian from any outsiders."

"But if they're walled in, how come the people don't starve?"

Charles smiled and said, "500 square miles is plenty of space for farms. They were smart about where they built the wall, and kept most of their natural resources, farmland, and mines inside. Millions of citizens were trapped outside the walls, but Emperor Chao had his resources, so he didn't care. The refugees fled to cities like Campton, trying to survive."

She was one of those refugees, tossed out and left to die. She'd seen other children starve, desperately begging passers-by who had nothing to give them. It was a miracle she and Zak had survived at all.

"After the wall was finished," Charles paused. "The Emperor killed the carbon elementalists, since they were his only threat left. He made sure every man, woman, and child with the ability to work carbon was killed. That's why you're so surprising, Emma, the world thought for years that he had succeeded. You proved that wrong."

#

The dock creaked beneath her feet as she hurried to keep up with Charles. This dock was cleaner and much larger than the one in Campton. Even after walking for several minutes, she still couldn't see the end.

Tall, stocky warhorses sauntered past them, their hooves clacking on the ground as they passed. Emma had never seen a horse up close. She marveled at how their long, braided black manes shimmered in the sun. They trotted proudly in straight lines, their attention set on the lead horse and their rider.

"Have you ever ridden a horse?"

Emma jumped at the question. She had been lost in thought while watching the horses.

"No, sir."

"John!" Charles bellowed at a nearby cadet. "Bring us a horse, we'll ride the rest of the way."

Emma's heart fluttered with excitement as the cadet brought over a brown-spotted mare. It towered over Emma, it's hot damp breath tickled her neck as it sniffed at her. Charles clicked his tongue as he took the reigns delicately in one hand. The horse bowed, lowering itself so it could be mounted.

Charles got onto the horse's back without hesitation and once balanced, reached a hand down to Emma. She put her hand in his and felt like a child as he lifted her onto the horse.

"Hold on," Charles said to her. "We'll be at the Academy in no time now."

The horse darted almost as soon as Emma was on. She gripped Charles' waist tightly as they galloped towards the city.

As they got closer to the heart of the city, Emma could hardly believe her eyes. She had never seen so many people at the same place before. It was even more crowded here than the King's Market.

Thousands of people hurried around in each direction, pushing carts and heading in and out of shops. They all looked well dressed and busy, out and about doing their business. The road was wider here too, and alongside it were perfectly trimmed hedges with bright blooming red and yellow flowers.

The roads were smooth and well paved, and on it, horses pulled carts of bricks, silk, and other goods. Houses and shops were several stories high, and each was beautifully painted to look crisp and clean. A smell of lavender seemed to linger in the air as they turned a corner deeper into the capital and passed a row of flower shops.

They turned down several roads, each leading down alleyways that twisted and turned between the buildings. Charles led the horse confidently down the different paths as Emma tried to remember the route they were taking. She took mental notes of the quaint bakery with the blue windows, and the apothecary with the round door, but there were too many things to see. She almost wished they had walked, so that she could take her time to look at everything they were passing. The city made her feel more alive than she had ever felt before.

#

Sweat trickled from Emma's forehead and her heart pounded in her chest. She struggled to catch her breath as she stared up at the giant stone castle in front of them. Five towers reached into the sky, almost touching the clouds that whisked slowly by.

The windows were thrown wide open along the towers, trying to tempt the summer breeze. Emma wished she was inside, sitting near a window and looking out over the courtyard that stood between her and the building. It was a huge, circular courtyard with immaculately trimmed grass and beautiful flower bushes dotted amongst the yard. The air smelled sweet, like honey and roses.

Charles led their horse under an old stone arch into the courtyard. The horse's hooves clacked loudly as they made their way towards the far end of the yard. They passed several large iron cauldrons that were placed every few yards along the path. Emma tried to peek inside them, but she was unable to get a good view without losing her balance.

A small group of people in dark grey robes gathered at the far edge of the courtyard. They watched intently as Emma and Charles approached, whispering loudly as they stared. Emma was sure they were talking about her. She felt a lump in her throat as they pulled to a stop in front of the group of old men.

Charles leapt off the horse swiftly and held out a hand for Emma.

It felt strange to be standing on solid ground again. She placed a hand on the horse's side for balance. His warmth comforted Emma as she watched Charles shake hands with the robed strangers.

"Welcome, Captain," the shortest man said as he bowed. "We're happy to have you back."

The man turned his attention to Emma.

"It's good to meet you as well, young lady, we've all heard a great deal about you."

Emma wished she could disappear. She wasn't used to all this attention. Her cheeks felt hot as she forced a small smile.

"We should get straight to the test," Charles said. His voice was firmer than usual.

Emma stared straight at the ground, holding herself, trying not to shake and let her nervousness show.

The old man who had spoken watched her for a moment before smiling and placing a hand on her shoulder. She jumped slightly.

"It'll be okay," he said. "We just have to see your strengths. Then you'll join the other new recruits. You'll like them. They arrived yesterday from around the kingdom, so they're as fresh and scared as you are. You'll make new friends fast."

Emma wanted to trust this man's kind words. But she had been abandoned more times than she could count and was cautious not to believe anyone. In the past, the only person she trusted was Zak, but he wasn't here. She had to do this alone, so that he could be safe.

Maybe it won't be so bad. There are other elementalists here at least.

She looked up slowly and nodded as the man smiled. His friendliness made Emma feel a little safer as she followed him to the nearest cauldron.

CHAPTER 4

A clear liquid came up to the rim of the large black cauldron. Emma focused on it while she raised her left hand. The liquid moved with her, following the motions of her wrist and gracefully gliding through the air. It floated weightlessly as she pushed her palm upwards, mimicking the old man's instructions.

After a few gestures, the old man scribbled some notes on a small piece of paper and nodded.

Emma followed him as he walked to the next cauldron in silence. Charles and the others followed, watching with interest as Emma inspected the next cauldron. It held a pale yellow powder. She raised an eyebrow and looked up at the man, unsure of what she was looking at.

He smiled and made a note before responding in a low voice, "Calcium oxide."

Emma looked back at the powder and attempted the same routine. It was harder this time, but she still managed to do most of the movements. Once she was finished, the man made another note, and led her to another cauldron.

They continued this process over and over as they made their way to each test. Some cauldrons contained liquids, powders, metals, and stones. A few were made of a clear material with a lid fastened on top.

Emma had never seen anything like it, she wondered if the clear cauldrons were made of glass. These clear cauldrons held different colored gases that seemed to billow and dance as she worked them. She smiled as a red gas moved in waves at her command, it was beautiful the way the colors shifted as the gas moved.

Emma continued the routine at each cauldron, moving all the compounds that were presented to her until the last few. Some of them wouldn't budge no matter how hard she focused. She wondered to herself what made these different, but didn't give it too much thought. She was getting tired from focusing and by the end of the circle, she felt lightheaded and dizzy. The entire courtyard seemed to spin. Her body trembled and her stomach growled.

"Interesting, very interesting," muttered the old man. He inspected his notes, and gestured towards the large wooden doors behind them. "I have to think about these results. For now, go eat."

#

"Hey!" A voice called out from a group of recruits. "It's the Captain's pet!"

Emma looked up to see a brown-haired, pale-faced boy with his finger pointed at her. The boy wasn't much older than Emma, but he was significantly larger. She took a small step back as his laughter echoed around the small cafeteria. Several of the other children joined in. All Emma wanted to do was run away and go back to Campton.

Do it for Zak.

She composed herself and decided it wasn't worth getting upset over. She could handle being mocked. She'd dealt with it before. She trudged towards an open seat.

The boy moved the air around him and launched a small air ball towards her as he smiled at the small group. He sneered as it flung towards her. The other children laughed.

Emma reacted as soon as it left him, and as the air ball hurtled in her direction she instinctively pushed it away with a quick flick of her wrist. The ball crashed into the wall, leaving a small dent in the stone.

The boy's face flushed and he furrowed his overly bushy brow. He tried again and formed a tight rapid ball of spinning air. Once the air ball was opaque and almost as large as his head, he pushed his palms outward in a forceful, exaggerated motion towards Emma. The other children gasped as it ricocheted towards her.

Emma steeled herself for the blow. She could have pushed it away, but instead she hoped he would leave her alone if he thought she had been defeated. She just wanted to be left alone.

The spinning air ran over her like thousands of needles, sending her crashing to the ground. Her face landed sideways on the cold stone floor, and she felt a stab of pain in her ribs when she exhaled.

It was not the worst pain she'd ever felt, but she still grimaced with each breath. Her whole body ached and tears fell silently onto the floor as she tried to sit up.

A loud cracking noise echoed in the cafeteria.

Emma peeled her eyes open and peeked at the boy who had just attacked her. He was rubbing his cheek with a look of indignation at the boy standing next to him. Her attacker was almost a foot taller than this new boy, but the smaller boy's eyes burned with anger.

"Leave her alone," the smaller boy said sternly.

"Stay the hell out of this, Adam!" The taller boy shoved him, but Adam quickly regained his footing. "I'll take you down too, you little shit. Nobody hits me and gets away with it."

The taller boy swung a fist at Adam, who barely dodged it. He lost his balance as he lunged forward and Adam punched him in the stomach. The boy wheezed and spat as he slumped backwards, clutching his gut. Laughter erupted from the other children around them.

"Adam, John! ENOUGH!"

A middle-aged man wearing a long blue velvet robe stepped towards them. His feet clicked loudly on the floor with each step. Five badges were stitched onto his right sleeve. Each one was beautifully embroidered with different symbols that Emma didn't recognize. He glared at the children, his pointed jaw locked in a scowl as he approached.

Emma forced herself to stand up, gripping her ribs and letting out a small groan as she did. The room was spinning. Her eyes were red, and her cheeks still burned. The larger boy, John, laughed under his breath and watched her.

The man walked past the boys until he was standing in front of Emma. He stopped and stared at her. His gray eyes pierced through her, sending a cold shiver down her neck. She tried not to flinch.

"Look at me," he commanded.

Emma glanced up and met his gaze, his lips formed a slight frown.

"You're a member of the Royal Guard now. Never retreat. Never back down – from anyone. Do you understand?"

Emma nodded and looked down at her feet.

"Now, go sit down and eat. All of you!"

John scoffed as he turned to walk towards a table.

"John," The man snapped. "Haven't you embarrassed yourself enough today?"

John spun around defiantly towards the man and said, "I taught the carbon bitch where her place is, and I'd do it again."

Emma's heart pounded in her throat. John stared at her. For the first time in her life, she wanted to hurt someone.

"Well, John," the man said calmly. "I suppose you'll need to be taught a lesson yourself then. Dinner will have to wait. Follow me, children."

#

They were at the center of the Academy a few minutes later. Most of the children scrambled to find a spot that lined the platform in the middle of the room. Emma and John followed the man, who had introduced himself as General Vanderheide, onto the raised stone platform.

"This is the training floor for smaller battles," General Vanderheide said. "At the Academy you won't be expected to face more than two opponents at a time, and you'll have several elements provided for you." He gestured towards the cauldrons that lined the platform. They looked exactly like the ones used for testing.

The children strained to see inside the cauldrons, muttering amongst themselves about what was in them. Emma looked down as she climbed the steps behind General Vanderheide and John. It looked like dirt, water, iron, and a few other rocks and metals that she didn't recognize.

"The compounds lining the platform may be used during a duel as well as anything that you have on you," General Vanderheide said. "We are teaching you how battles work in the real world, but do not kill your opponent in practice. Getting them on the ground for 10 seconds is plenty."

The children stared silently at Emma and John. Some shuffled anxiously, but most stood completely still.

General Vanderheide gestured at the two of them.

"Stand on opposite ends and bow to each other."

Emma walked to the far end of the platform and tried to convince herself to be brave. She had to show General Vanderheide that she was worth training.

Emma bowed and waited for the signal to start.

You can beat him.

John gave a half bow, and immediately started his attack.

He threw his arm in the air and three air balls flew towards her. She barely managed to dodge them as they zipped past her.

Her heart raced and pain coursed through her ribs from earlier.

John prepared to strike again and Emma braced herself to defend. She knew she'd have to attack, but she wanted to be careful since she didn't have any real experience fighting.

John focused his energy on manipulating the air around him, muttering to himself as he did. She tried to focus on what he was doing.

I wonder if he only works with air.

His attacks appeared to be limited to air balls shot at rapid speeds, and although they were dangerous, Emma realized that if she could dodge them she could start attacking him back without much effort.

Another air ball, larger and more powerful than the earlier set, whipped towards her. She deflected it and sent it hurtling above the crowd of children. A petite blonde girl screamed as it shot over her, narrowly missing her shoulder.

Emma looked around her and saw a pile of iron bricks, and an idea hit her. She shifted her footing, and focused her attention on the iron as she motioned with her right hand upwards. The iron shifted into an almost liquid form as it rose out of the cauldron. Carefully, Emma manipulated the iron into a long, thin cord before launching it towards John.

John jumped back, almost falling off the edge of the platform as he tried to avoid the iron cord pushed in his direction. He began rapidly flinging air balls at the iron, but they weren't strong enough to push the metal back.

Emma lurched forward and wrapped the metal up around his legs and torso until it bound his lower half. John was outraged, screaming loudly and launching more air while he struggled to keep his balance.

In desperation, John sent air balls hurtling around the large room. A few crashed into the wall and sent small shards of stone cascading to the ground. Air darted in all directions, creating chaos and panic among the children. John had lost control of himself and was firing at random while struggling to break free. He reminded Emma of the caged dogs she'd seen in Campton, howling and thrashing.

She tightened the iron around John, forcing him to lose his balance and slam to the ground.

John exhaled deeply, the wind knocked from his lungs. His face was red and sweat beaded at his forehead. He tried to push himself up with his arms as he screamed obscenities at Emma.

"Stay down!" Emma screamed as she tightened the iron cords around him and forced them to wrap around his arms as well. John was pinned. "It's over."

John struggled, but was not strong enough to move the iron.

"Emma has won," General Vanderheide declared. "This fight is over, everyone return to dinner and don't let this happen again."

Emma nodded and released John.

She had won, and the victory felt good even though she knew there would be consequences later.

#

Emma flopped down on her bed in exhaustion - the other children had gone for dinner, but she had gone straight to her room. She needed some time alone to calm down.

Sleep washed over her within minutes and dreams of Zak and John took over. She tossed and turned until she woke up in a cold sweat. Emma sighed and wiped herself dry before crawling back into bed. She didn't go back to sleep, but just stared at the ceiling, thinking about her brother until a knock on the door startled her.

She forced herself up off the low bed. The stone floor was cold on her bare feet, and the white walls made the room seem small and uninviting.

Her hand wrapped around the doorknob, and she cautiously pulled the heavy oak door open.

"Good morning, Emma." It was the old man that had led her from cauldron to cauldron, testing her. He stood casually outside her door, dressed in a plain brown coat and long pants. "I have finished reviewing my notes from yesterday. The King wants to meet you and go over the results."

Emma frowned and took an unconscious step backwards.

She stuttered, "Why would the King want to see me? I'm just a refugee."

"A refugee with amazing skills."

"But I don't understand --"

"You will. Get dressed and I'll take you." He handed her a long green dress and closed the door.

Emma pulled the dress on over her head and looked at herself in the thin mirror on the wall. It fit her fairly well, but was a tad large. She had never worn a dress before, but she imagined meeting the King required some formality. She fumbled with her shoes and ran her fingers through her knotted hair. It had been several days since she had brushed it, and she was suddenly self conscious.

As soon as she was presentable, she opened the door and stood for the old man's inspection. He looked her over and nodded.

"Good," he said. "Follow me."

They walked in silence down the twisted staircase that led out of the tower. Emma assumed that behind each door was another room like hers – cold, white, and empty, waiting for new recruits to fill them. She wondered how many rooms were in this tower, and if the other 4 towers were the same. If she had the chance, she decided she'd go exploring and find out someday.

"Sir," Emma said quietly. "Why aren't you in a robe like the other teacher? I heard that master elementalists wore robes that showed their skills at all times. Was that not true?"

"It is true, but I'm not a elementalist," he said. "And I'm not a sir. My name is Dominic, and I am a chemist. Chemists don't wear robes unless we're conducting Academy tests or teaching lectures."

His voice was gruff, but she liked the way he pronounced things. He sounded different than the people in Campton.

"A chemist?"

"You've never heard of a chemist?" He looked at her with one eyebrow raised.

She shook her head.

"We can't work elements like you can. We need tools to do it. But, we aren't limited to certain ones either -- once we know which tools to use, we can work anything."

Emma beamed. "So you can work carbon too?"

"No." He paused. "At least, not in the way you can. I can manipulate carbon with my tools, but it is slow, and takes years of study to master."

Emma thought about this. She'd never had to study before; everything came naturally to her.

"Most of the other children had to study to work the elements as well, like chemists do."

Emma was confused, "What is the difference between an elementalist and a chemist then? Do elementalists just not need the tools?"

"Essentially. Some are more gifted and don't need to study to do the basics, like you. However, most need to learn how the elements fit together, to form bonds and structures. This is where chemists come in. We teach them important facts, like how two Hydrogen and one Oxygen make water. They focus on the pieces, rather than the whole. It makes them weaker than someone like you." He chuckled softly to himself.

Emma paused for a moment and said, "Because I can move things without knowing what goes into them?"

"Exactly. You are rare for that alone. When you add in your carbon-working skills and your extraordinary rank, your talents are unbelievable."

"Rank?"

"You'll know soon enough," he said as he stopped walking. "We'll speak over it with the King."

The door in front of them was massive. It was made of thick oak and had a giant deer head carved into it. The eyes seemed to stare back at Emma as she ran her hand along the intricate cuts in the wood. Behind these doors was the most powerful man in the world, and he wanted to speak to her. She gulped and took a deep breath as the door swung open.

A voice boomed from inside the room, "The Royal Chemist Dominic Hurlbert and Royal Guard recruit Emma Wilkinson have arrived."

CHAPTER 5

Sunlight flooded the room, spreading a warm orange glow along the polished marble floor. A rich, warm cedar smell put Emma at ease as she breathed in deeply. She had never been anywhere near a place this luxurious.

Mahogany beams stretched into the air up to the arched royal blue ceiling. Thick velvet curtains hung the length of the walls, elegantly tied back with golden silk cords. There was a gentle dusting of snow resting on the trees just outside the windows. Emma thought it contrasted nicely with the massive fireplace that crackled near the throne.

Every part of the throne room made her feel out of place. It was exotic and foreign to her; she would have been more comfortable meeting with someone in the slums or a dark alley.

King Terril sat in the throne with his legs loosely crossed. He took a large drink from his silver goblet and handed it to one of the several servants beside him. Emma had never imagined that the former war hero would be quite so fat. The buttons on his tunic strained against the fabric, letting small patches of his cream colored undershirt show through.

"Ah, they're finally here!" The King said in a raspy voice. "So tell me, Dominic, is she as good as Charles claims?"

Dominic stopped a few yards in front of the throne and bowed. Emma did the same.

"Yes sir," he replied. "I tested her and ranked her abilities. Shall I read her results?"

The King nodded and took another drink of his wine.

Dominic looked at Emma and said, "We rank each element from 1-5. 1 is a novice, while 5 is a master. To do our tests, we use simple compounds to determine the ability of each individual element. In order to work a compound, one must be at least a novice in each element comprising more than roughly one percent of its total make up."

Emma nodded. She got the general concept despite being a little confused on what it meant to have one percent of an element.

Dominic handed the King a small piece of parchment, and then slipped one to Emma as well.

5: Carbon
4: Iron, Oxygen, Hydrogen
3: Nitrogen, Copper, Gold
2: Silver, Zinc, Sodium
1: Platinum, Neon, Calcium, Potassium, Sulfur, Magnesium

"She also possesses the ability to work compounds that she has never encountered before, without knowing the chemical structure."

The King closed his eyes for a moment after reading the parchment several times. He set it down and pushed himself off his throne.

"Amazing." He said while walking around Emma. He twirled a finger through his beard as he looked at her. "Show me."

Emma looked up at him, confused. What did he mean, show him?

The King pointed to a large candleholder next to the throne. "Turn it into a sword."

Emma nodded and focused on the metal candleholder. She shifted her weight onto her back leg and leaned into the movements, pulling with her hands and commanding the metal.

The candle crashed to the floor as the metal began shifting shape and moved towards her. It floated through the air as it morphed into a short sword with a small handle. Emma reached out and grabbed it.

The King smiled as he took the sword from her. He inspected it from hilt to tip, nodding as he checked it over.

"That is quite impressive," he said. His voice trailed off like he was lost in thought. After a few moments he said, "Dominic, I want her trained as an assassin, not a guard."

"But, sir --" Dominic protested.

"My orders are final," the King said sternly. "You have four years to train her fully, and she'll need a partner. I trust you can pick one of the other recruits."

"Yes, sir," Dominic said, defeated.

"Good. Emma, you'll be the best in my army someday. I'm looking forward to seeing your skills after you've been trained." He smiled. "You may go now."

Dominic bowed once more and quickly led Emma out of the throne room. Her mind raced as she thought about what had happened. She had so many questions. She didn't know where to start.

Dominic remained silent as they hurried out of the room and through the halls of the castle. He led her back towards the Academy through crooked hallways and down twisted stairways.

Suddenly, he spun around and looked at Emma, his cheeks flushed.

"Do you have any idea what's happened?"

Emma shook her head.

"The metal you worked back in the throne room was steel. No one – nobody we've encountered – can work it like you did. He's ordering me to train you to become his personal assassin, and there is nothing Charles or I can do to protect you from it. You're a sweet girl, but soon..."

He choked on his words as he spoke, his voice shook.

Dominic whispered, "You'll be the best weapon in his army. I'm sorry."

#

Surprisingly none of the other children jeered or laughed at her as she walked into the small dining hall. She heaved a sigh of relief and focused her attention on the assortment of pastries on the nearest table. The room smelled of sweet bread and raspberries, and the children chattered amongst themselves as Emma sat down in an empty chair.

Emma grabbed a roll and slathered on a hearty helping of butter and jam. She was starving. It had been almost a full day since she'd last eaten. Her mouth watered as she took her first bite of the flaky roll.

After she had finished eating her second roll, she realized that Adam was watching her from across the table. Her cheeks grew warm as she blushed.

Adam laughed and said, "Did Dominic tell you we're going to be partners? It's exciting, he told us you're going to be an assassin and asked for volunteers to train as a medic. To follow you around and make sure you don't die."

Emma looked up, sure he was mocking her. A huge grin was plastered on his face, and he seemed genuinely pleased to be her partner. She remembered how he had fought with John yesterday. Maybe she could make friends after all.

"You're stronger than any of us," he rambled. "It's awesome that I'll be your partner. I'll probably learn a lot more this way, even if it is riskier. Although, John was pretty pissed. He's petitioning right now to be an assassin as well."

The other two boys at their table laughed at the comment.

The girl sitting at the end said, "Why should Emma be the only one to train as an assassin? If John gets approved, I'll be his partner. We'll get to be just as strong as you someday."

She flashed a playful smile at Emma.

"I doubt that!" Adam laughed. "Did you see her yesterday? She kicked John's ass."

"True, but she's scared," the girl said as she smiled to herself. "You can see it in her eyes."

"No, she isn't!" Adam protested. "Not everyone feels the need to show off all the time."

Emma spoke up, "But I am scared. I don't want to be here, but I have to be. I'll do what I must, but I'm not the person you think I am. You should find a different partner."

She felt ashamed to admit it, but it was true. The only reason she had come was to help her brother. She didn't want to be anyone's weapon.

Adam looked at her, and shrugged. He took a big gulp from his pewter cup and said, "Nope, I've decided. You're stuck with me."

He winked.

No boy had ever winked at her before.

Emma shifted in her seat uncomfortably. Adam was a handsome boy, about a year older than she was. He had dazzling green eyes that seemed to stare through her. It made her want to sink into her chair and disappear. She had never been particularly interested in the attention of boys, and she hoped he didn't want to be her partner for other reasons.

Heavy boots clacked down the hallway towards them, echoing as several people approached the dining hall. Emma looked up as Dominic and General Vanderheide stepped through the arched wooden doorway. Dominic looked particularly thin compared to General Vanderheide, who was quite muscular and still in the prime of his life. Dominic looked like an old man who had lived a hard life, leaving him frail with wispy gray hair.

"We've discussed your skills and decided teams for training," Dominic announced. He stood up straight with his shoulders held back. "Come line up, boys on one side, girls on the other."

Emma noticed for the first time that there were an equal number of boys and girls. She hadn't really looked around at the other children much until now. She realized that most were her age, although some seemed older by a year or two. The other girls were taller than she was, and more developed. They were all in pants and loose cotton tunics.

The girl from earlier stood in front of Emma. She was about the same height as her, but had a more muscular build. She looked confident. She focused on the instructors intently.

"Teams will be broken into three categories," General Vanderheide said. "Some of you have been chosen for the Royal Guard. Others will go into the Navy. A few of you will be trained into Diplomatic Relations as assassins."

A small bloom of hope blossomed in Emma's chest that the King might have changed his mind. Maybe she would be placed into a different team. She didn't want to be a killer, she'd do better in the Navy or the Royal Guard. The death of the guard in Campton haunted her and woke her up at night in cold sweats. It was like his shadow followed her and entered her thoughts whenever she was alone. She couldn't sleep without seeing his face or hearing his final breath.

"Ryan and Eva," Dominic's voice cut through Emma's thoughts. "You will be trained into the navy."

A small group of cheers and clapping came from the lines of children. A short, stocky boy with sticky black hair, and a petite blonde girl with long legs stepped forward. They were directed to the left of Dominic and General Vanderheide. Emma's heart raced as Dominic continued down the list.

"Greg and Jessica, Royal Guard." Two more children stepped up and took their place. Dominic continued to name off pairs, and Emma's hope began to turn to panic.

"Emma and Adam. Diplomatic Relations."

Every head turned to look at her, and she froze. Her body wouldn't move forward. She stared back at Dominic. Everything felt cold and distant, like this was all a dream.

Adam smiled and walked up to form a third line. He waited patiently for Emma to join him.

Hesitantly, Emma made her way to the front of the room and stood beside him. The girl from earlier was the only person left standing without a group.

"Harper," Dominic said. "You and John will also be in Diplomatic Relations. He will join training with all of you later."

Emma was relieved that she and Adam weren't the only would-be assassins, but wished anyone but John had been chosen. He hated her, and she knew that he would make the next four years more difficult.

"I want you to get settled into your rooms tonight," Dominic said. "You'll be separated by your training groups, and also by gender. Follow me."

#

Their bunks were in plain white rooms like the one Emma had stayed in the previous night. The only exception was a small window that looked out over the courtyard. Two beds sat on opposite ends of the room, made neatly with white linens and a few small pillows. Everything looked crisp and sanitary. There was a single, small bookcase under the window, and a mirror hung on the back of the door. Despite all of these things, the room felt empty and cold.

"Do you care which bed you get?" Harper asked.

Emma shook her head. It made no difference to her; they were practically identical.

"Okay," Harper smiled. "I'll take the one on the right then."

Harper started setting her things out on the bed and said, "Do you ever actually talk?"

Emma just shrugged and sat down on her own bed. She'd never really talked to other children her own age. She'd been perfectly happy with just her and her brother.

She stared out the window at the courtyard, the afternoon light made the grounds sparkle as the light dusting of snow melted.

"It was amazing," Harper said as she sat down. "Watching you yesterday. I wasn't making fun of you or anything at breakfast."

"Thanks," Emma said. She felt herself blush.

Harper was filled with excitement now. "Isn't it amazing? We're going to be trained as assassins! That means we get special training that the others won't.

We'll be going on missions in just a few months with our teachers. We'll be unstoppable!"

Harper's enthusiasm shocked her, and she wasn't sure how to respond.

"But we'll be doing it to kill people," she said. "Doesn't that bother you?"

Harper looked down at her hands and said, "I've seen people die before, but I've never killed anyone. I think it'll be okay if they're bad people. I could kill bad people."

Silence hung over them. There was a tension in the room, a mutual awkwardness that sat between the two of them for several minutes.

A knock saved them from the uncomfortable silence. Adam entered the room, his trademark grin plastered on his face and his messy hair covering his forehead.

"Your room looks like ours!" he exclaimed. "John wasn't there yet, but they said he'd be back soon, Harper. We're supposed to walk down in teams and go to our first lesson with Dominic."

Emma stood up and exchanged an awkward glance with Harper, who nodded promptly. She hurried with Adam out of the bunk room.

They half ran down the spiral staircase, their footsteps echoing on the stone as they turned down several corridors. Emma followed Adam's lead.

How does he know the route so well already?

They passed through a study room that was filled with leather bound books and red velvet chairs. Emma wished she could stop and read through them, lounging in the comfort of the chairs.

She spotted a fireplace tucked away in the corner as they hurried past, its flames flickered dully at her. Her brother had always wanted a fireplace. She wondered what he had done with the sack of gold she'd left him. She imagined him in a stone house, with a small yard in the city center. He would have a dog that sat next to him as he read his new collection of books. Emma had saved up for months to buy him a storybook on his birthday last year. She'd bought him a book about a knight saving a village from an ogre. He loved tales of knights fighting for their kingdoms.

Lost in thought, Emma tripped and tumbled knee-first into a doorframe. Adam turned and reached out his hand to help her up.

"Watch your step. Don't want to miss our first lesson."

CHAPTER 6

Adam and Emma walked onto the courtyard that
had been used earlier for testing. Other children stood
at attention. Dominic stood in the center of the
courtyard looking at the children. They wore three
colors of uniforms. One group wore purple and gold,
the colors of the Royal Guard. The Navy group wore
dark blue and silver. Emma and Adam wore all black
with no embellishments.

John and Harper jogged out of the building shortly
after Emma and Adam had lined up. The black
uniforms they had on made John look harsher and
more intimidating. A chill crept down Emma's spine.
They hadn't even started yet and she was already
dreading working with him.

The courtyard was quiet. Everyone stared at
Dominic. He didn't say anything. Minutes went by in
silence.

"Are we going to get started?" John blurted out.

"Yes, John." Dominic looked at him and smiled,
"Today we're learning about patience, and how crucial
it is for all of you."

Emma's shoulders dropped. She was not a patient
person.

Dominic gestured behind him at a fountain of a
man riding a warhorse while holding a sword. The

water trickled out of the tip of the sword and ran down his back.

"The test today is to recreate the statue out of stone. You will each get a chance to show your skills, and at the end of the day, you will be graded on accuracy. This will take a great deal of patience to get right, and you'll have to work with your partner."

He looked around at the children. "One of you from each team, go grab a piece of stone."

Emma walked over to a pile of square stones, fresh from the quarries. She picked a medium piece that had sharp, clean edges and lugged it back to Adam.

"How do we want to do this?" Adam asked.

Emma examined the stone. She could probably work it directly.

"I'm going to try something," she said.

She shifted her weight onto her back leg slightly, and concentrated on the stone.

It jolted and cracked, and a corner fell off.

"Shit."

"What?" Adam asked. "Can't you do it?"

Emma balled her fists and frowned.

"No, it's too delicate. It'll break before I can make the shape."

Adam examined the stone, leaning over to pick up the crumbled corner with his fingers.

"We could try breaking it slower," he said. "By using something else, like water or air?"

Emma looked around. She noticed that some of the other children seemed to be thinking the same thing.

She watched a pair from the Navy move water

quickly over the stone. After a few minutes their concentration failed and the water splashed to the ground. They sighed and started again.

"Let's try it," Emma said, turning her attention back to Adam.

Adam changed his stance, and focused intently on the fountain. A ball of water came towards him. He smiled a large, toothy grin.

"This could work."

Emma mimicked Adam's movements and grabbed a small amount of water from the fountain. She tugged it through the air and forced it over the small piece of stone in a swirling motion.

"How can you do that so smoothly?" Adam asked. "Don't you lose focus on the elements?"

Emma furrowed her brow and replied, "I don't know what you mean."

"You know, tracking the hydrogen and oxygen?"

"I just look at it as water..."

Adam dropped the water he was working with, and it sloshed around his feet.

"How do you do that?" He was practically shouting with excitement. "Can you teach me?"

"I... don't know how I do it. I just do."

"Well...someday we'll have to figure it out so you can teach me too."

Adam gathered the water up again and continued. He looked disappointed.

She felt guilty, like she was hiding something from him, but she didn't know how she did it. It just worked.

They continued to work for several hours in

silence, slowly carving away at the stone. Adam dropped his water several times, and each time he grew more frustrated. His posture shifted faster and his movements were less controlled by the end of the fourth hour.

"I give up!" It was a boy that had Royal Guard colors on. He sat on the ground with his head in his hands.

Another hour passed, and the outline of the statue was finally taking shape. It was messy, but identifiable. Four teams had quit now. John and Harper were almost done; John stood to the side while Harper took on the final details alone.

"How does she do that so quickly?" Emma asked.

Harper whipped the water back and forth in thin strips, chipping quickly away at the stone. Her control was breathtaking. Their statue was almost complete.

"She grew up on a Navy ship," Adam said. "Her dad is a naval officer."

Emma looked confused. "Then why didn't she want to go into the Navy like her dad?"

The water splashed to the floor, slipping from Adam's control as they talked. He swore under his breath and grabbed more from the fountain.

"Maybe she didn't like living on a boat?"

"I suppose," Emma imagined living on a boat, sailing the oceans with her dad and Zak. They'd stop once in awhile at islands they passed, each different from the other. She would have given anything for that life. She made a mental note to ask Harper about her life later.

Dominic walked slowly towards them, watching

61

intently as the two of them worked.

He closed the distance that separated them and said, "Emma, describe what you're doing. In detail, please."

"Using water from the fountain to carve the stone, sir?" She replied. Something about his voice made her question her answer.

"Adam, please expand her answer."

"We're working hydrogen and oxygen, sir."

Dominic sighed, "More specifically?"

"Two parts hydrogen and one part oxygen." Adam looked at Dominic for approval.

"Good. Show Emma the proper posture for working hydrogen."

Adam's weight shifted back on his right leg as he crouched down low with his hands extended out in front of him. His elbows were bent at a slight angle, and he held his palms up as if he were cradling something fragile.

Dominic smiled.

"And oxygen."

Adam repositioned himself, relieving his rear leg of some of his weight. Now, he was less crouched and his arms bent closer towards his stomach. His palms faced down.

"Perfect." Dominic was pleased. "Now, finally, water. Or, two parts hydrogen, one part oxygen."

His stance shifted into a mixture of the two earlier poses. He bent down, not as deep as when he was working hydrogen, but at a larger angle than when he was working oxygen. His palms curved forwards. It was a blend of the two postures, and Emma realized that this was how he had been standing most of the day.

"Do you see why I'm showing this to you, Emma?" Dominic asked.

Emma shrugged, unsure of what to say.

Adam laughed and said, "Your posture hasn't been right all day is why."

Emma felt a heat swell up in her and she snapped, "I'm still doing better than you!"

She clamped her mouth closed as soon as the words came out. That wasn't like her. Her cheeks blushed with embarrassment and she lowered her head.

"You've got a gift, but your natural talent can only get you so far," Dominic said calmly despite Emma's sudden outburst. "Try it again with a better stance. You'll see a difference."

Emma watched the way Adam stood. He was like a statue, perfectly balanced. Even his clothes seemed to stop moving in the wind as he worked. She copied his posture and concentrated once again on the water. In a quick, swift motion, she pulled a long cord of water towards her from the fountain. Each fingertip seemed more in tune with the motions now. Even though she wasn't used to standing like this, she noticed that she had more precise control of the water. It felt like an extension of her hands.

"That's much better," Dominic said. "Once you learn the chemical composition of something, you can work with it in the correct stance. It is an art to be able to find the balance between these stances. You have to know the chemical structures and be able to concentrate while working. It's difficult, but the difference it makes is amazing."

Emma marveled at the difference her stance had. Dominic was right; she was noticeably better now.

Why couldn't he have brought this up hours ago? We'd be done by now.

John and Harper walked over, their statue finished. John's arms were crossed and he had a smug look on his face, as if he had completed it by himself. Harper stood next to him with a small, humble smile. She was the opposite of John, and Emma wondered how they could possibly be good partners.

"We're done." John said.

"You mean Harper is done," Adam replied with a laugh.

Harper giggled and John turned a bright, angry red. He glared at Adam.

Dominic broke the tension by saying, "Go inside, I'll inspect it once everyone else is done as well."

Harper waved good-bye cheerily as they turned to leave.

#

The past few months seemed to run together in a blur.

Every day started the same, training at dawn with Dominic, then lunch in the dining hall. Every day after lunch they worked with General Vanderheide until dusk. Then, if they weren't too exhausted they'd get dinner before falling asleep. It was the same thing each day with no breaks.

Dominic had been focusing on their stances and changing their situations daily. He threw new challenges at them whenever they mastered something. They never knew what was coming.

General Vanderheide had been teaching them survival skills and camouflage. Unlike their lessons with Dominic, these training sessions were only for the assassins, so only the 4 students were present. He taught them to build shelters, start fires, and skin wild game.

Today they had a quarterly exam to test their progress. Emma and Adam would be dueling John and Harper. She had seen how much progress they had made, and she was nervous that her and Adam might not win.

Emma walked alone down the spiral staircase towards the center of the building. Her mind raced as she thought about the upcoming exam; John would be particularly aggressive, they hadn't dueled since the first day they'd met. Even though they were on slightly better terms now, she knew he still wanted to win more than anything.

Adam waited for her at the bottom of the stairs. He was always ready before she was. Emma had started looking forward to seeing him each day, he always seemed so happy. She wished she could be like that.

"Ready for today?" he asked.

"I suppose so," she said. Her hands shook next to her side.

He looked at her hands and chuckled. "You don't look like it."

She blushed and shoved her hands in her pockets.

"At least John can hate both of us now," Adam said with a cheeky grin. "After we kick their asses."

Emma laughed. His confidence made her feel a bit more at ease.

Adam reminded her of Zak sometimes. Both of them could see the bright side of things, even when she didn't. It was comforting to have him as a partner. She couldn't imagine how lost she'd feel without him here.

John and Harper paced the length of the room and pointed out different substances. They spoke to each other in hushed whispers, and barely glanced up as Adam and Emma entered the room. Dominic and General Vanderheide stood on one edge of the platform.

Dominic looked up from his notebook and said, "Good, we're all here. Let's get started."

Emma took a deep breath as she stepped onto the platform. She gripped the railing, her pale knuckles contrasting the dark wood. The memory of her earlier duel with John made her ribs ache.

It'll be okay.

Emma felt like a different person than she was a few months ago, but something about this duel made her nervous. She felt disadvantaged, despite how much she'd learned these past few months. John had made an astounding amount of progress, and Harper was just as formidable. She had the skills of an assassin with hydrogen and oxygen already. No one could defeat her when it came to working with water.

Emma wasn't sure if she was strong enough to beat Harper or John alone. Not without using carbon and seriously injuring them, but she wasn't willing to do that. In her training she'd been working to master other elements so that she wouldn't need to kill on all her future missions. She knew this took away one of her main advantages today.

As they lined up across from each other, Emma noticed how calm Harper looked. Her long blonde hair was tied in a neat ponytail and rested delicately on her back. She was elegant, fierce, and deadly. Emma wished she could look that confident, but instead she clasped her hands behind her back and tried to keep herself from shaking.

"Okay," General Vanderheide said, interrupting Emma's thoughts. "It's time. Bow to each other, and then begin on the count of three. Dominic and I will be judging you and determining your continued training based on your performance as a team. Understood?"

They all nodded and bowed.

"One, two, three --"

John let out a wild, piercing screech.

Emma clasped her hands over her ears just as a pulse of air slammed against her like a wave. She barely managed to keep herself from falling off the edge of the platform. Adam grabbed her tricep to help her regain her balance before turning back to face John and Harper.

Adam immediately struck back with a dramatic push of air towards their opponents. He pushed them back slightly, but John was prepared and blocked most of the blow. It gave Emma enough time to regain her footing.

John's face and arms were bright red and his mouth twisted into an unpleasant scowl, he was determined to win this time. Harper stood calmly and gracefully shifted into her water stance.

From the corner of her eye, Emma saw a column of water rush upwards out of a nearby cauldron. It moved like it was alive, pulsating and growing in size as Harper pulled at it. Emma braced herself.

The water struck down on them hard, soaking both Emma and Adam. Had she not noticed, Emma would have had the wind knocked out of her. Adam, quick as always, noticed Harper's stance as well and had prepared for the wave. He was standing upright and turned to Emma with a smile as if to say, "Fight back already!"

Emma knew she had to do something.

She grabbed the nearest element, iron, and formed a handful of small pellets while dodging the air balls John blasted towards them. Ten iron pellets floated weightlessly in front of her; she launched them at John's chest.

"Shit!" John yelped in pain as a few of the iron balls struck him. He took a step back and rubbed his chest where one pellet had hit him.

Adam laughed, but lost focus and took a water whip to the back. He yelped as Harper rolled her eyes and chuckled.

Both Adam and John were temporarily buckled over in pain.

Emma didn't want to fight Harper, but she wasn't going to back down either. If Emma didn't act quickly, John would be back up on his feet. Emma stepped forward into a stance.

Harper mirrored her, stepping forward as well. She shifted low into a position that Emma didn't recognize. They stared intently at each other for a few moments before making their attacks.

Emma tugged at the air around her to form a small tornado. She pushed it towards Harper's feet to make her lose balance. Harper struggled, but kept her footing; she was strong and crouched low to offset the swirling winds.

Emma could not see what Harper was working, but based on her movements she assumed it was helium. If it was, she didn't have long. Once the helium was around her, she'd faint from the lack of oxygen.

Noticing that John was almost back on his feet as well, Emma let go of the winds at Harper's feet and grabbed the nearby water. She forced it above her in a large wall, and thrust it forward at John and Harper. It struck hard, knocking John off the platform and distracting Harper from the helium. Harper frowned as she re-balanced herself.

In a series of quick movements, Harper took part of the water from Emma's control and froze it beneath their feet. The three of them were now locked in place.

Blood dripped from her forehead and trickled down her cheeks, but the corners of her mouth twisted in a smile. She wasn't going down without a fight.

Adam looked up, still partially dazed, and said, "You've got this, Emma!"

"Ha! Not yet you don't. I've still got a trick up my sleeves."

Harper stood calmly and moved her hands in small

circular motions. The air around them started to vibrate, and water rose up from off the ground around them. Small droplets of ice crystallized in the air, vibrating quickly along with the air as they grew in size. In a sudden burst, they rushed towards Emma, pelting her with hard chunks.

Emma screamed in pain as the ice cut her skin. Her whole body seemed to be on fire, and every breath she took was agonizing. The ice was so cold it burnt the parts of her skin that were exposed. A fist-sized mark covered her left cheek, and her arms were covered in bright red welts.

Emma fell to her knees, the ice around her feet shattered as she collapsed.

#

Emma felt weak as she stared up at Adam. Drops of blood ran down his shaggy blonde hair and dripped to the ground.

She tried to stand up, but her ribs cracked and it felt hard to breathe.

"Slow down, Emma," Dominic looked at her as he whispered. "Good thing you heal quickly. It should only take a day or two to get this frostbite cleared up, but the ribs may take longer. I'll have nurse Burleson take a look."

"Frostbite?" Adam said. "From those ice balls?"

Harper laughed nervously, and shuffled her feet. Her forehead had a long streak of blood across it, and a small stream trickled down her cheek. It looked unnaturally bright against her alabaster skin.

"That was a trick I learned, actually," Harper said. "It wasn't ice, it was liquid nitrogen meant to look like ice. Kind of a nasty trick..."

She reached out and grabbed Emma's hand in her own.

"I'm sorry. I really didn't think it would be this bad. Let's go see the nurse."

"It's okay," Emma replied. "I gave you a nasty mark too."

Harper laughed. "This? This is nothing. John gives me worse with his stray air balls during training. He needs anger management or something."

"Where is he by the way?" Emma asked as she looked around.

"Yeah, where did he go?"

"He must have left right after the fight got done," Adam said.

"I suppose we should just go then," Harper said. "Gotta get healed up before our first mission."

They turned and walked off of the platform and out of the room. Emma struggled to keep up with them as they walked down the halls towards the medical wing. She wasn't disappointed that they'd lost, but all she wanted to do was sleep. Her body ached and her mind was racing, replaying the fight in her head and what she should have done differently.

Adam noticed that Emma was limping and gently wrapped his arm around her waist. She rested most of her weight against him. The warmth of his skin was soothing, and Emma was grateful for his help as he half dragged her to the nurse.

CHAPTER 7

Emma held her breath as the train pulled into the station.

She had never seen a train before, much less ridden one, and was amazed by the loud noises and puffs of smoke that came from this strange machine. The train was much larger than she had imagined, and a lot noisier too. It reminded her of a long carriage, with iron wheels that rode on tracks made of hard pounded steel.

She pressed her palms over her ears to drown out the sound, but it was still overwhelming. Her head pounded.

"Don't worry," Adam said. "I'll protect you."

He winked at her. Emma normally loved Adam's cheekiness, but today she was fed up with it. This was serious; it was their first shadow mission. They couldn't mess this up, their future training depended on it.

How is he so calm?

"Okay, this is our ride," Charles said. "All aboard."

Emma followed Charles onto the train and Adam stepped up closely behind her.

It was smaller on the inside than Emma had imagined, even with just the three of them, their cabin was packed so tightly they could barely turn. A small price to pay for the added speed, she supposed. There were no benches in their cabin. Charles told them that the better cabins towards the front had cushioned seats for when the King and his dignitaries rode.

"Aren't you a dignitary?" She had asked. "Being the captain of the guard?"

Charles frowned and explained that he was an ordinary man, who had simply worked hard to become a Captain. He said there was nothing dignified about him or his past.

Emma looked out the window as the train started to move. They'd be in the Baldock Marshes in three hours. If they rode a horse, it would be almost a day's ride. Walking would take weeks.

"Who are we meeting again?" Adam asked.

"A man named Pon. He'll be the one taking you on the mission," Charles responded. "Normally, you'd be given a rendezvous point and be expected to meet him on your own, but I also have business with him. And besides, it's a nice bonding trip, right?"

He laughed deeply, which pushed Emma closer into Adam. She nudged back, trying to maintain some personal space in the cramped cabin.

The train jolted from side to side as it began to move. The pungent smell of coal burning filled the air as the train rushed down the tracks. The landscape seemed to swirl into blurred shapes, whizzing past and gone before Emma could process what they were.

Soon, the city was left behind them, and within a few minutes they were beyond the walls of Portishead. The passing fields were covered with a thin layer of snow, and spotted with rowan trees. Clouds raced across the sky, casting shadows across the ground.

Emma had never seen such perfectly thick white clouds before. It made the winter scene look clean and crisp. It was soothing to watch the clouds shift gently and move with the wind.

"Are you ready?" Charles asked.

Emma pulled her attention away from a cloud that resembled a strange fish with wings, and shrugged. She didn't think she'd ever be ready to be an assassin. It still didn't feel right to her, killing other people for political gain.

Charles clapped a hand on her back, and said. "You'll be fine. You're practically a prodigy."

Adam smiled and said, "Plus, you've got me as a partner."

The three of them laughed, causing their cabin to shake.

They were just entering the forest that stretched between Portishead and the Baldocks. The trees seemed to appear alongside them out of nowhere. The view of the sky was replaced by the trunks and leaves of hundreds of old oak trees.

Emma feared that the train would strike an outlying branch as they rushed through the narrow passage in the woods, but to her relief it never happened. She couldn't believe how precisely the tracks had been laid, and how well the trees had been cut back. There was barely enough room for the train, but it continued dutifully down the path without delay.

#

The day had turned misty, and the steps off the train were slippery. Emma carefully followed Charles onto the rickety wooden platform.

Chipped red paint clung to the small building that resembled an abandoned barn in front of them. A crooked sign hung above the door that read 'Baldock Marshes - Train Stop 217'.

Emma's legs felt weak as they stood on the level, unmoving platform. She had grown accustomed to the shaking of the train, and now it felt odd to be on stable ground.

They watched as the train pulled out of the station behind them.

It grew quiet.

Charles tapped his foot anxiously, his arms crossed over his stomach.

"It's just like Pon to be late," he muttered to himself. "Even at the Academy. Always late."

Suddenly, Emma felt a tap on her shoulder. She jumped and let out a small scream. A small man with short black hair looked up at her. He was thin and quite pale, and dressed in all black.

He frowned.

"She screamed," he said to Charles in a flat tone. "Why hasn't she been trained not to scream?"

"Dammit Pon!" Charles broke into a large toothy grin. He thrust out a hand to shake Pons. "It's good to see you after so long, but did you really have to test them this early? Let's at least get dinner first."

Pon shrugged.

He looked over Adam, and jabbed at his arms and stomach intrusively.

"You need to feed this one more."

Adam and Emma exchanged looks of uncertainty. This was the person that was supposed to teach them? He didn't seem like a master assassin. Emma had expected someone tall, muscular, and much scarier looking. Not a judgemental little man like this.

They walked into the building that looked like a barn, and as they got closer, Emma realized it was larger than she had initially thought. The building extended underneath the entire platform, and the small barn was just the entrance. It smelled musty and the air felt stale.

Two guards stood alert on either side of the door, nodding as Pon and Charles passed them. As they stepped in, Emma and Adam stared in amazement at the inside of the building. It was massive; a staircase led down from the front door, and immediately opened up to a series of hallways that extended underneath the train's platform. The massive building was painted a dull gray, with bare wooden floors. Doors lined the hallways, each labelled with a series of numbers. Their feet echoed down the hallway as they walked to door 37.

The door creaked open. A small flicker of light escaped from a large torch that hung on the tiny room's wall. A table with a pitcher of water, several glasses, and a large piece of paper sat in the middle of the room. Four chairs waited for them.

"We'll be going over the plan in here," Pon said. "Take a seat."

Each of them grabbed a wooden chair and sat down to look at the paper laid out in front of them. It was a hand drawn map.

Baldock Marshes - Western Pass

Several roads ran the length of the paper, combining into a single, wider path that led through the patches of marshland. There was a ten mile stretch where only one road led through the marsh before it branched off into smaller roads again.

The legend showed that the marsh was typically very deep, with some areas reaching just over thirty feet in depth. A series of symbols indicated the depth and conditions of the marsh.

"Our mission will take place here, along this road that passes through the swamp." Pon pointed at the long single road that Emma had noticed on the map. He tapped his finger at a place where the legend indicated deep waters and narrow roads. "We'll be stationed here at daybreak tomorrow. We may need to stay there for several hours...maybe all day."

"Who is the target?" Charles asked.

Pon dug for something in his pocket, and pulled out a sketch of a middle-aged man in an intricate robe adorned with jewels. His face was narrow and stern, and his cropped black hair was partially hidden by a large velvet hat.

"Viscount Befauex," Pon replied. "He has been assisting the rebels by providing supplies and sanctuary. This is a threat to the King, and a critical mission for the realm. I don't understand why the King assigned you to it for your first shadow mission...but, I was ordered to take you with."

His voice was bitter, all his earlier playfulness was gone as he looked at Emma and Adam critically. After a few moments of silence, he smiled half-heartedly.

"Oh well," he sighed. "Maybe you're better than you look."

He grabbed a piece of charcoal out of his pocket and drew a circle around their mission's location. He added an arrow that pointed to the southern bank of the path.

"We'll be camouflaged and hiding here. When the time comes I'll tell you the specifics, but for now just know that you have to stay hidden. It could destroy the mission, and jeopardize our lives if we're spotted."

Emma's hair stood on end at the nape of her neck. A chill crept down her spine. She had never expected to be thrown into such a serious mission so soon after joining the Academy.

I'm not ready for this.

She had no choice; she had to continue. She'd sold herself to the King for Zak. After this was all over, she'd request a report on how he was doing from Charles. She consoled herself imagining Zak living comfortably.

"Tonight, all you two need to do is eat and get some sleep," Pon said, interrupting Emma's thoughts. "Your rooms are out the door and to the left, your dinner should already be in there. I need to speak with Charles alone."

Adam looked at Emma, his eyebrow raised questioningly. They wondered why they weren't being told the specifics yet, or why they were being dismissed.

"It's all right," Charles said. "I'll see you when you get back tomorrow."

With a smile, Charles got up and opened the door for them. He pointed down the hall and nodded as they walked out. It would be a long day tomorrow, and Emma hoped she could sleep.

#

Their mission was simple; kill the Viscount, James Befauex, while he was traveling between towns. He would have a team of guards, all ready to die for him, but unnecessary casualties were to be avoided if possible.

Emma fidgeted as they sat waiting in the tall marsh grass. She remembered their exercise in patience at the Academy; that was nothing compared to this. Her body was submerged, and her joints ached from the cold. The water seeped through her thin canvas clothing and coated her in a thin layer of grime. She desperately wanted a warm bath.

The mud on her face hardened and cracked as the day dragged on. It itched and she desperately wanted to scratch it, but she'd been forbidden from moving unless absolutely necessary. Pon had described in too much detail how to use the bathroom without moving her whole body. Emma was appalled at the idea.

The sun started to set. A warm orange glow bounced off the water. The area around them was still, except for the occasional croak of a bullfrog. The only movement was the gentle swaying of the marsh grasses in the wind. They reminded Emma of long tufts of yellow hair that delicately swayed back and forth.

Suddenly, a light clicking echoed on the road leading towards them.

Horses.

The Viscount's carriage was finally making its way down the path. The sound of hooves grew louder and the shadows of the lead guards stretched ahead on the path in front of them.

Closer.

They needed to be closer.

Anticipation coursed through Emma like a surge of electricity. She'd never imagined being put in this position, but the urgency of the situation made her anxious. Part of her wanted to stop Pon. But she imagined Zak in the city living happily. She couldn't let him down. She couldn't let herself down, she'd come this far. She had no choice.

The first guard was in front of them now, watching diligently for any signs of danger. He looked right past where they were hidden.

Hooves stomped down a few inches from Emma. She focused hard on remaining still.

Guards appeared all around them on the path, their footsteps rivaled the noise of the horses. The guards wore plain gray tunics with emerald scabbards on their waists. They marched forward, watching the path as they maintained formation. Soon they were all visible along the road.

Twelve men guarded the plain wooden carriage. Even with so few embellishments, and several knots and dings, the large patrol of guards made it obvious that the carriage carried someone important. They wanted to be as low key as possible in order to avoid attention, but the large assortment of guards made that impossible.

Out of the corner of her eye, Emma saw the water ripple slightly around Pon. It would be impossible to notice from the path; his hands moved so delicately that the water barely quivered.

It's time.

The large brown draft horses that pulled the carriage walked confidently. Emma watched as Pon pulled the earth from beneath their feet slightly, causing them to misstep and falter. He continued to move the ground a few inches at a time, watching as they stumbled.

The closer of the two horses reared in frustration. It stomped down hard a few inches away from Emma's face. She gasped and jumped backwards instinctively.

SHIT.

"What was that?" A guard yelled from behind the carriage..

"I heard it too," the guard beside him said.

Pon glared at Emma, his expression was hard and furious. Beneath his thickly layered camouflage, his eyes burned like fire, drilling into Emma. He had managed to move the earth enough to make the carriage fall into the water. It was lying on it's side, slowly sinking, but two guards had heard Emma. Their mission would not be as simple as they'd hoped.

The two guards that had heard her approached her hiding spot, their footsteps grew louder.

Her heart pounded in her throat. Her first mission, and she had ruined everything.

NO! I can fix this.

Her thoughts raced as she scrambled to focus on the two guards. She forced all of her energy into making their bodies do what she told them. She gripped the elements inside them, and pushed them away from her like she had done so many times with water.

They're just elements. I can move them.

She shoved them as hard as she could.

They tried to yell, but she forced their mouths closed. She pursed their lips together as they shook their heads trying to fight her grasp.

Emma's temples pounded as she concentrated on turning the men around. It would look suspicious if they walked away from the sinking carriage, and she had an idea. The carriage was sinking deeper into the water as the lead horses tried to swim away.

Emma pushed them towards the chaos of the carriage as they struggled hard against her control.

Now.

In one last desperate movement, she thrust the guards against the carriage. She pinned them underneath it as Pon manipulated the water to sink the carriage faster. He needed to ensure that the Viscount would drown before anyone could rescue him.

Emma struggled not to faint as she worked the water around the two guards. Her head buzzed and she felt dizzy, but she had successfully gotten them trapped under the carriage. Now she just to hold them there.

She had to kill them, they knew someone was hiding in the swamp.

She'd worked water countless times before, but never under pressure like this. The guards kicked, trying to get themselves above water as they gasped desperately for air. She tightened the water around their ankles, holding them in place. Tears ran down her face as she concentrated on the water around them.

They pushed against her, trying with all their strength to swim upwards. Their hands scraped along the carriage, grabbing at anything they could. She imagined the two guards, fighting with everything they had to resurface, but she held them down.

They have to die.

Finally the struggling stopped. The water was calm. Emma sensed their lifeless bodies floating in the water.

Her knees went weak.

Water rushed over her face as she fell backwards, down into the swamp. Adam managed to catch her and pull her back above water without drawing any more attention to them. The guards were busy clawing at the carriage door, trying to rescue the Viscount. He was already dead; Pon had made sure of it. Now they just needed to wait until the guards left, defeated.

CHAPTER 8

"You almost ruined everything!" Pon was livid. His screams brought Emma to tears. "How could they send a girl who can't even hold still?"

"I'm sorry," Emma muttered.

She knew she'd messed up during the mission, but Pon's anger scared her and made her feel terrible. She wanted to run away.

She didn't remember what had happened after she fell back into the water. Adam said he had held her up until the guards left, and then carried her back to base. She was grateful for him. Pon might have left her to drown.

"Pon," Charles said. "Calm down. She's still a recruit in training. At least she thought on her feet and fixed it."

"Fixed it? By the skin of her teeth!" His face was bright red and spit flung from his mouth as he yelled. "We could have been spotted. If we were, we would have had to kill all those guards! They would have known it was a planned assassination. Do you know how mad the King would have been?"

"But you didn't have to kill those guards and they don't know it was an assassination," Charles said calmly. "The mission was successful. It still looked like an accident."

Pon yelled something unintelligible. He glared at Emma.

"She's dangerous and reckless! I won't take her with me again."

Pon turned, his hands balled into tight fists as he stomped out of the room. His footsteps echoed down the hall, and his frustrated shouts continued until he had left the building.

Emma sat down on a nearby chair and put her head down on the table. She couldn't keep herself from crying any longer. She gasped for breath between sobs.

Charles walked over and set a hand gently on her back and looked down at her.

"Pon overreacted," his voice was soft and calm. "He's got a wicked temper. You did fine for a new recruit."

Adam sat across the table from Emma and said, "You did the best you could. Don't beat yourself up."

"We'll work harder on your training," Charles said. "Then next time you'll be perfect."

Emma looked up slightly and wiped the tears and snot from her face. She nodded.

Charles rubbed her back gently and whispered, "But, between us three. I think you were amazing out there."

Emma raised her head up the rest of the way and stared at Charles. Her eyes were bloodshot from crying.

"How was I amazing?" She cried. "I killed two men that didn't need to die. I held them under the water while they struggled to breathe. I felt their lives leaving them, disappearing, as they fought against me. They wanted to live, and I murdered them."

Her voice cracked and she began to shake.

"How can I live with myself?"

She broke into deep, heart wrenching tears. Her body heaved as she breathed heavily in between sobs. She couldn't stop herself. All she could picture was the last few moments of those guards' life, the way the water had moved as they had struggled, and then suddenly stopped when they took their last breaths. She had held them down as the water rushed down their throats. Those few minutes would haunt her for the rest of her life.

#

The train ride back to Portishead seemed longer than the one that had gotten them here. The silence in the cabin was suffocating, and the tension was palpable. Charles and Adam had attempted to console Emma, but nothing could make her forget the dying guards. She kept wiping away tears as the train bounced along the tracks.

Charles remembered back to when he first killed someone. He was only 15 years old when a thief had broken into his parent's house. He remembered his mother's screams as he ran down the stairs to find her lying on the kitchen floor. Blood pooled around her as a taller, older boy stalked over her, Charles had never felt so much rage.

He'd leapt at the boy, and smashed his head hard against the ground. The thief tried desperately to defend himself and drove a small knife deep into Charles' arm.

Charles ignored the pain, his focus was on beating this intruder that had hurt his mother. The world went red as he punched the boy repeatedly in the face.

His eyelid split open and blood coated Charles' hands.

He didn't stop. He kept hitting the thief over and over, rage coursing through him as he beat him until he stopped breathing.

"Charles!" His mother screamed. "Stop!"

His life had been a cold, distant fog for days after that. His mind replayed every second of that day, and nothing felt real for weeks. His mother made a full recovery, but Charles vowed that he'd never let anyone hurt his family again. He joined the navy later that year.

At the landing platform in Portishead, Charles stood still for a minute and enjoyed the warmth of the sun. The cool winds blew lightly from the south, just barely rustling the flags above the station.

Charles escorted Emma and Adam back to the Academy library where floor-to-ceiling mahogany shelves lined the walls with books. The center of the room had plush couches and chairs, cherry end tables, and several blankets laid out across the surfaces. The rich scent of wood and old books washed over them.

"Take a seat," Charles said as he plopped down on a brown leather couch. "I'm sure they'll be here soon."

"They? Who are we meeting?" Adam asked as he sat in an armchair with a sigh. The chair was huge and could easily fit two people.

Charles smiled. "You'll see. I've set you up with a new trainer. He's not an assassin, but he's amazing at strategies."

Adam nodded and looked around the room. The library was empty except for the three of them. Charles sat alert, his legs crossed loosely and his face slightly flushed. On his upper arm was a scar that his tunic failed to cover in his relaxed posture.

"How'd you get that scar?" Emma asked pointing at his bicep. "I've never noticed it before."

Charles chuckled and said, "Being a Captain means I've seen my fair share of fights. This was from my first."

Footsteps echoed towards them with a steady tapping against the marble floors. Emma and Adam perked up in their chairs and watched the doors as the strangers approached.

Two men entered the library. One was about Charles' age, but shorter and stockier. He had a birthmark that covered the entire left side of his face. The other was closer to Emma's age. He was tall, with dark brown hair and emerald eyes. Both wore plain black tunics and pants, with golden emblems adorning the sleeves.

"You're late," Charles said as he stood and shook the older man's hand.

"Jason was being debriefed by his father," the older man said. "Apparently, this is something rather important?"

"Yes," Charles said. "Training this team is very important to the King, as I'm sure you know, Geoff."

Charles waved Emma and Adam over to join them.

"This is Jason," Charles said gesturing to the younger man. "He'll be training you both. He's very experienced and will help you achieve your full potential. Since your training is top priority, he'll be taking you on advanced missions with him once you're ready, and teaching you some crucial skills you'll need for planning assassinations."

Jason smiled at Emma and Adam. He shifted back and forth on his feet as he looked them over.

"I've heard a lot about you two. We'll start right away with drills tomorrow morning, it won't be like the training you've done so far with Dominic."

Adam raised an eyebrow.

"Will we still be learning about elemental structures then?" Adam asked.

Jason laughed quietly, seemingly amused by his question.

"Oh, you'll still be learning it," he said. "But now you'll have a little more on your plate than most trainees. Dominic will still be around to help you, so will Vanderheide. But I'll be taking over your training where it actually matters from now on."

Adam frowned and slumped his shoulders slightly. He didn't appear pleased with this plan.

Jason laughed and patted Adam condescendingly on the shoulder.

"Don't worry, I won't hurt you too much," he said. "Meet me tomorrow at 5 in the courtyard. We'll start immediately."

He took his hand off Adam's shoulder and walked out of the room.

Geoff bowed quickly to Charles and hurried out of the room after Jason.

"Well, I guess you'd better get to bed then," Charles said. "The Prince doesn't like when people are late."

Emma and Adam exchanged a look of confusion.

"That was Prince Jason?" Adam asked. His voice shook slightly.

Charles smiled and gave a quick nod.

"He's one of the best," he said. "Even King Terril admits that. Your training with him is crucial, so don't slack off."

#

The room was bathed in a pale golden light from the early sunrise. It had been months since Emma had woken up this early, but today was all about making a good first impression. She had to arrive on time and be prepared for whatever the Prince was going to throw at her in training.

A knock on her door jolted her to attention. She stood up and walked to the door.

Harper rolled over and tossed the blanket over her head as Emma passed her. She grumbled quietly about how she didn't have to wake up for another hour or so.

A bright light from the hallway shone through as Emma opened the door. Adam stood outside with a large lit torch. It cast a warm glow around the room and bounced shadows off of his strong cheekbones, showing off the masculine structure of his face that Emma had never noticed before.

"You ready?" he asked, his voice raspy with sleepiness. "Don't want to keep Princey waiting."

Emma scowled at him.

"You're going to get us in trouble," she snapped. "What's your problem with him anyway?"

She hurried to pull on her socks and shoes, dodging the pillow that Harper lobbed across the room towards her. Emma stuck her tongue out at Harper's back, but knew that if their roles were reversed she'd have done the same.

Emma wished she had time to bathe; her skin felt sticky from sweating in her sleep. She'd been having nightmares since their mission, and on several occasions had woken Harper up with her night terrors.

Every night was the same. She saw the guards dying in front of her, fighting desperately for their lives. Harper had asked her about it a few nights back, but she cried each time she tried to describe the mission. It was something she knew she'd have to get past, but the idea of having to kill again plagued her.

"Okay," Adam said as he tapped his foot impatiently. "You're ready and looking more beautiful than ever. Let's go."

Emma jumped to her feet and punched Adam in the arm. She had grown used to his taunts, but couldn't think of a witty comeback this early.

They walked quickly down the staircase, hurrying to the courtyard to meet Jason. Neither of them knew what to expect. They just assumed it would be more difficult than anything they'd done before.

It was a bitter cold morning; the frost clung to the shrubs and grass like a thick blanket, bouncing the morning light into their eyes. Emma could feel her lips going numb within a few steps of going outside into the wind. Her stomach lurched uncomfortably.

Jason stood in the middle of the courtyard waiting for them. He was surrounded by twenty guards, all standing at attention. Their hands rested uniformly on their sword hilts, all eyes rested on Emma and Adam as they entered.

Jason's face was stern and strong, but his eyes had a kindness in them that made Emma feel at ease. Adam, on the other hand, walked stiffly with his arms locked to his sides. He was obviously not excited.

"Good," Jason said as they approached. "We're going to be doing field work in the woods today. I'll be taking you into the forest outside of the city, where you'll begin a very important aspect of your training: learning how to conceal yourselves. This is a skill that will be crucial in your missions. It can be the difference between life and death, so take it seriously."

Jason paused and made eye contact with them to make sure they were paying attention.

"You will have thirty minutes to find a hiding spot. After that, the guards will come to look for you. Your objective is to stay hidden until sunset."

Jason looked back at the guards behind him.

"If you find them before then, feel free to rough them up a bit. Just don't cause permanent damage."

He walked up to Emma and looked at her. He was close enough that she could smell cinnamon on his breath.

"If they find you, do not hurt them," he said. "I like my guards. They're quite lovely people. I'll be watching the entire time. Understood?"

Emma nodded.

Jason smiled and turned towards the courtyard's exit. He waved a hand for them to follow.

CHAPTER 9

They passed through the city market just as bakers began setting out their freshly baked goods for sale. An old woman laid out rolls on a table and Emma's stomach growled as she imagined biting into the warm, fragrant dough. Her mouth watered as they walked past.

Jason continued to lead them forward until they had passed through the western gate of the inner city walls. Emma noticed that Portishead was similar to Campton; a large wall separated the dignitaries from the common people. Only a few merchants and bakers were allowed within the innermost circle. This kept the poor as far from the Palace as possible.

As they went further from the palace, the houses began to look smaller and more run down. They passed through several alleyways that were littered with waste, and they scared away a few stray cats as their boots clicked on the cobblestone streets. Emma wondered how big this city was. It seemed to go on forever.

After almost thirty minutes of walking, they reached a large stone archway with a dirt path. Trees lined the route on either side, towering well above them, their tops brushed up against the edge of the wall.

Emma looked out into the woods. Walking between the trees seemed almost impossible; the trees to the sides of the route grew so close together that it was hard to see more than a few feet.

Jason stopped just outside of the archway and turned around to face them. He gestured towards the forest ahead of them.

"Here we are," he said. "This archway separates the city and the forest. Once you step through it, you'll have approximately thirty minutes to find your hiding place. I'll be following you, observing your movements and making notes on how you approach this task. But I will not interfere with whatever may happen until sunset. That's about ten hours from now, and even though I'll be nearby, you're on your own until then."

Emma swallowed.

It's going to be a long day.

"So, if we can hide the whole day we can just go back without any problems?" Adam asked.

Jason grinned. "That's right."

Emma felt a chill crawl up her spine. Something told her it wouldn't be that easy.

"Shall we?" Adam asked.

"Sure."

Jason gestured ahead, and told them to begin.

"Where do you think we should go?" Emma asked as they walked into the forest.

Adam pointed to the top of the trees. "Up?"

Emma craned her neck up. "But how do we get up there?"

"Leave that to me," Adam said as he began moving the air around them.

He pulled a circle of air towards them and flattened it out into a small platform. It was spinning quickly at the base, but he managed to hold the uppermost layer steady.

"Get on."

Hesitantly, Emma stepped up onto the platform. She prepared herself to jump down in case something went wrong, but it was surprisingly stable.

Jason got on after her, and finally Adam followed, carefully holding his hands steady as he moved. Emma admired his concentration as he pushed downwards, forcing the air below them against the platform. With a few quick motions, they began to rise into the treetops.

Emma was confident in Adam's abilities, but couldn't help feeling a little scared that they would plummet back to the ground. Adam didn't give her much time to worry though. In a few minutes, he had managed to get them to a small limb that branched out of a tree several hundred feet above the ground.

Emma leapt off of the air platform and onto the solid branch of the tree, sighing with relief as she grasped to its trunk.

"Okay," she said. "What now? Should we go in deeper?"

Adam thought for a minute, his fingers rubbed against the sides of his chin as he looked around them.

"I think we should go in a little further, and see if we can find a tightly packed grouping of limbs to hide in. Can you work the tree limbs?"

"I'll try."

She fixed her concentration on a nearby twig with several leaves. She could feel the carbon, and the nitrogen and oxygen buzzing inside it. She could feel it pushing back against her, just like those two guards had during their final breaths. She gasped and stepped backwards, almost falling off the branch. Adam grabbed her arm just in time and pulled her into him.

"Are you okay?"

"Yeah," she said back, still a little shaken. "It just... feels alive. It shoved back in my direction, like it didn't want to be worked."

"You remembered the guards didn't you?" Adam looked at her sympathetically.

Emma stared at the twig and nodded.

You can do this.

She focused on the twig again and grabbed onto it's chemical structure, pulling the whole of it towards her. She reached out a hand and touched a bright green leaf gently with her index finger.

"Awesome," Adam said under his breath. "Now we can hide in the trees better. Let's find a spot where you can wrap a few branches around us. That'll add cover."

They hopped from branch to branch, heading deeper into the woods. Adam carefully brushed the snow off the branches to hide their footsteps as they went. It took about ten minutes before they saw a gathering of branches that stretched out like a small fork. It would be just large enough for them to perch on.

Emma crafted a cover around them out of the branches and worked quickly so that they wouldn't be caught by the guards as they entered the forest.

Jason hid himself a few hundred feet behind them, quickly disappearing from their sight.

Once Emma was happy with their hiding spot, she and Adam balanced themselves delicately on the branches and waited. They hoped that everything would work out fine, and that they could hide here in silence until sunset.

It was over an hour before they saw the first group of guards walking up and down the area below them. Emma held her breath as one of them passed beneath them. He continued past them and Emma exhaled with relief; it was almost noon and they still hadn't been found.

Today may go smoothly after all.

Suddenly, a shock rocked the trees around them and a loud bang went off several hundred feet to their right. Emma had to keep herself from shrieking as she grasped onto the branches for support. The tree shook under her.

Another shock bent the tree several feet to the side before it rebounded back. Emma felt sick to her stomach.

Four more blasts went off in the next minute, each louder than the previous. Bile crept up in her throat. She pressed her tongue to the roof of her mouth; it was a trick she had learned to stop herself from throwing up. The tree continued to shake violently, and it took all of her strength to hold on and stay quiet.

It was several minutes after the blasts before Emma finally calmed down again. She hoped that the guards had moved on to a different area for a while, and allowed herself a few moments of relief as she sat down on the branch beneath her. She felt well hidden and safe, what would it hurt if she rested a minute before the guards came back?

Adam whispered under his breath in an urgent tone. "We have to move. Now."

"Why? We're hidden fine," Emma protested as she pushed herself up.

She smelled smoke coming from below them. Her eyes bulged as she saw the first few licks of fire crawl up the tree towards them.

"Shit," she said, just louder than a whisper. "This way."

She jumped to a branch behind them, being careful not to slip on the light dusting of snow that was melting from the heat of the fire. Her feet barely gripped as she lunged from branch to branch, trying to out pace the flames that followed them. It felt like the fire was forcing them in this direction, pushing them deeper into the woods.

Emma was sure that a guard was feeding the flames towards them, trying to flush them out. She wondered if Jason had let the guards know where they had hidden, as a test to see what they would do.

Adam slipped and let out a quiet yelp as he fell several feet to a branch below them. Emma turned quickly and rushed towards him as the flames threatened to overtake him. She saw a guard in the distance behind them. She was right; he was guiding the flames.

Emma reached Adam just as the flames grew around them. Instinctively, she worked the air surrounding them to keep the fire away. They gasped for breath, and struggled not to cough.

Emma tossed Adam over her shoulder and jumped down to a lower branch, hoping to escape the growing fire.

Adam leaned into her, and grabbed her around her shoulders.

He whispered, "I think I twisted my ankle."

Emma swore under her breath and continued climbing downwards. It was almost too much for her, carrying Adam as she half jumped, half fell down the trees.

She felt faint. She needed to rest and catch her breath.

Water.

The thought shot through Emma's mind quickly as she heard the faintest sound of trickling water. There must be a river near them. She looked around desperately.

The slightest hint of blue broke through the trees to her left. It was a small river that ran through the forest. If she moved quickly, she could change course and get there without the guard noticing her.

She made a run towards the river, carrying Adam as they moved to outrun the flames. She hoped to have enough of a head start to evade the guard if he noticed their change in course.

The river rushed quickly over rocks and tree roots beneath them. Small white tipped waves carried branches and small stones down the river. It was faster than Emma had expected, but she had no choice. She jumped in, pulling Adam with her.

The cold water soaked through her coat. She shivered violently. If the water wasn't moving, it would have been covered in a thick layer of ice. Emma forced herself down under the water, holding onto Adam as she fought against the current.

She cried out as she smacked into a sharp rock. Pain coursed through her back as she felt the rock cut her body. Her vision blurred, and she could feel herself going numb. Instinctively, she pulled the oxygen out of the water around her and made a bubble around them. It was harder to maintain a bubble of air in the water as they kept getting knocked against the rocks. The river continued to whip them downstream.

Just a little further.

Emma clung onto Adam while maintaining the cushion around them. She desperately counted the passing seconds as they shot down the river. After two minutes, she couldn't hold on any longer.

In a strong push, she forced them out of the water and onto the snowy beach. Her body shook and she couldn't feel her fingers.

Adam looked pale and was barely breathing. His ankle was swollen and the skin around it was a dark purple.

We still have to make it at least two more hours. What am I supposed to do?

She looked up into the trees. Surely Jason would call off the training with Adam injured like this. Emma's teeth chattered. They were also at risk of frostbite in this cold. She waited, hoping Jason would call out to them.

Nothing in the forest moved besides the gentle swaying of the leaves in the freezing winds and the river behind her. She knew that Jason was watching to see what she'd do. It soon became clear that she was on her own.

Emma remembered something Dominic said to her before she went on her last mission: "Your powers are just as good for healing as they are for killing." What had he meant? She imagined the blood pumping through them. If she sped up the particles in the blood, it would get warmer and they could avoid hypothermia. In theory, she could save them from the cold, but if she did it wrong, they would die. It was a dangerous gamble, but she didn't see any other way.

Carefully, Emma focused on the blood flowing through Adam's chest. She placed her hands on him and closed her eyes. She forced the blood to warm up under her touch. His face turned bright red, and heated up quickly; it was as if he had a fever. She backed down a little and maintained a delicate balance.

Several minutes passed before Adam was able to sit up. Emma's head hurt from all the concentration, and she began to try the same technique on herself. Her blood flowed unnaturally hot through her veins, but she could feel life returning to her sore, frozen limbs. Feeling gradually returned to her fingers and toes.

"Any sign of guards?" Adam asked, as he looked around. He seemed more coherent now.

"Not yet."

"Then we need to do something about these soaked clothes. If we take them off, I can dry them with a few blasts of air."

Emma blushed and shook her head. She would rather freeze than take her clothes off in front of him.

Adam frowned.

"It's either that, or you freeze. I promise not to look."

Emma didn't like it, but decided he was right. The wind was making her cold again, and she knew she didn't have the strength to warm them both until sunset.

"Close your eyes," she demanded. She glared into the trees, hoping that if Jason were nearby he would also take the hint as she stripped down.

She hung her wet clothes up nearby as she clutched herself, trying to keep her body warm as she stood unprotected in the cold.

"Okay," she said as her teeth clattered. "Hurry up."

Adam pushed air throughout her clothes and dried them in a few seconds. Emma grabbed them as soon as he finished and quickly pulled them on. They were still cold, but at least now they were dry. She turned around so Adam could undress as well.

"Emma," he said. "Can you hang my clothes up? I can't stand."

Emma turned around to grab his clothing from him. She tried to avoid looking, but couldn't help noticing the muscle definition in his legs and abs as she grabbed his pants and shirt from him. She blushed and hurried to hang his clothes.

"We need to move again. They're bound to be here soon," Emma said as Adam put his clothes back on.

Adam agreed with her, and tried his best to walk with her support. They hobbled into the woods away from the river and Emma wondered if they could manage much longer. Their bodies were weak from lack of food and the biting cold. They'd have to tough it out until Jason collected them.

They heard a branch break above their heads.

A guard jumped towards them, sword in hand, poised to strike at them.

Emma noticed two tree roots stretching out before her. She dropped Adam onto the ground. He groaned in protest, but if her idea was going to work, she had to act quickly.

She craned her neck down and focused on the two roots that lay beneath her feet. They were long and stretched out about ten feet. She focused all her energy on the roots and began to form a cage around the guard who had almost reached them.

He was trapped in a cage made from the thick, gnarly tree roots.

Emma smiled, pleased with herself for how quickly she had executed that. She watched as the guard swung his sword at the roots. It was futile; the cage was double-layered, and there was no way he could cut his way out before they were several minutes away.

Emma grabbed Adam again and continued to hobble deeper into the woods. They were getting closer; the sun was falling on the horizon, casting a warm, hazy orange over the forest. It had been a long day, but they would be done soon.

Darkness covered the forest floor, the last few minutes before sunset. Emma was exhausted. Her adrenaline waned, and she collapsed to the ground. Adam sat himself up against her.

"I suppose we're almost done," he said. "Jason should be here any minute."

"I'm glad," Emma said. "I can't take it anymore. I feel like passing out."

Just as Adam was about to reply, they heard shuffling come from around them, the sound of several sets of footsteps approaching through the forest. Emma was too tired to get up and defend herself.

She watched as the guards closed in on them in the darkness, hoping that they would bring news that their training was done for the day. It was almost sunset already; they had to be finished....

Maybe this is the final test.

A guard lunged towards them, his sword extended outwards. Emma barely dodged as the blade sliced across her cheek. She cringed in pain and realized that they weren't done yet.

With all of her remaining strength, she pushed the nearest tree around them like a shield. She was exhausted, but within seconds they were enclosed in the tree. She had formed a hollow space with just enough room for the two of them to be crammed next to each other. It was pitch black.

She felt Adam's breath, weak and warm against her neck. They were both too exhausted to fight; they would have to pray that the guards couldn't break in.

It felt like hours before a knock on the tree startled Emma. Jason's voice was muffled through the bark of the tree; she could barely understand him.

"Come out," he yelled. "Day is over."

Emma hesitated. She felt the hot, sticky blood on her cheek. She was worried that it was a trap, but she desperately hoped it wasn't; her whole body ached.

She pushed aside a small portion of the tree around them, just enough so that Jason and the guards could pull them out.

Jason's green eyes stared down at her as she laid on the ground. A smile crossed his face.

"Good job. You put on quite the show."

Emma felt her eyelids droop and the world fell into blackness as two of the guards lifted her and carried her back towards the city. She fell asleep before they'd put her into the back of the carriage. What felt like the longest day of her life was finally over.

CHAPTER 10

Training continued on, days turning to weeks and weeks turning to months. Soon it had been two years since Emma had come to Portishead. It was hard to believe that time had passed so quickly.

Jason had pushed Emma and Adam to their limits, giving them new challenges and making sure they worked hard. He was a tough trainer, but they learned quickly.

Emma's determination amazed Jason. He marveled at the fire that burned inside her. In all his years at the academy, he had never met anyone quite like her. She was strong and had the passion of a warrior. Her attitude reminded him of how he had been after his father dropped him into the Academy at only five. He had been eager to prove himself and make his father proud.

It took Jason six years to realize he'd never be strong enough in his father's eyes. His father had always been hard on him, difficult to impress and rarely expressed any form of emotion. So Jason decided he'd be powerful in his own way. His mother taught him that if he couldn't be the strongest, he could be the smartest. He was intuitive and had a natural ability to read people and understand their feelings. People trusted and valued his opinions, just like they had once with his mother. It was something his father lacked.

He knew his mother would love Emma. Emma was kind and persistent. Her heart was full of love for her younger brother. Everyone at the Academy respected that this was what pushed her forward. Jason had made sure she received regular updates on Zak's life, or at least as many as his father would allow.

Today, they were going on a larger mission than usual, joined by John and Harper. Their task was to protect the King's convoy as he headed to the nearby city of Chelmsford on diplomatic business. According to reports, the threat of an attack from the rebels was low, but it was better to err on the side of safety. Recently the rebels had grown bolder, and the roads were more dangerous for the nobility.

Jason waited for them about a mile from the Academy on an empty street. In a few hours, people would be bringing out their tables, setting down their spools of silk and freshly baked breads in front of them. It was good that they were leaving early.

Jason tapped his foot as he looked down the narrow street. In the distance, Adam and Emma turned around a corner towards him. John and Harper followed close behind. The four had learned to work well together, but there was still resentment and anger. Jason had tried to get the teams to become friends, but with John, he had settled for civility.

Harper was so different from her partner. John was always brooding and making snide comments, but she was friendly and smiled easily. Her quick wit and sharp remarks often made Emma giggle. He wished he could be their friend and joke around like they did, but he had to stay professional as their trainer.

"Good morning trainees," Jason said. They met his gaze and gave a low bow. "Today, the five of us will head to Chelmsford. The King will be in his carriage, and he'll be conducting some important diplomatic discussions with the Duke once we get there. Any questions?"

They shook their heads.

"Then let's go. It's a bit of a walk and we'll be navigating through a forest, but today should be a breeze compared to training."

The night sky started to blend with the orange light of the sun. The sun peeked above the rooftops and bathed the city in a warm, peaceful glow.

Jason almost hoped they would run into trouble so he could show off his team to his father. Something like a small group of rebels. He knew this was a dangerous thought; if anything were to happen to the King...Jason pushed the thought out of his mind.

No, today needs to go smoothly.

Jason noticed how attentive Harper and John were, they observed the area around them diligently. They scanned the fields and marshes alongside the road, remaining alert for any signs of danger.

Emma and Adam were almost the opposite. They trudged along, their eyes on the ground as they shuffled their feet. They weren't normally like this; he knew they were tired, but they were years into their training and he expected more of them. He'd have to wake them up.

He fell behind the group and moved to the back of the carriage quietly. He kept his focus on Emma and Adam as they walked listlessly.

With the flick of his wrist, Jason made a few rocks move near Emma's right foot. She looked down, puzzled, but didn't seem to think much of it. He did it again more forcefully. She stopped walking to look at the jumping pile of rocks that followed her. She looked around, trying to find who was causing this as she waved at Adam with her left hand. He snapped out of his daze and looked around.

Jason stopped moving the rocks and suppressed a childish laugh to himself.

Maybe now they'll pay attention.

He returned to the front and caught up with them.

"How's everything going up here?" He asked.

Emma glanced down at her feet, and replied slowly, "It's fine."

"Good, let's hope it stays that way once we get into the forest. There are a lot more places for bandits to hide once we're inside, and even if they don't know the King is in the carriage, it's obviously being used by someone important."

Emma nodded and looked ahead.

"I've never been in a forest like this before," she said. "The trees are so dense and dark. They look angry."

Jason looked up, he supposed the forest did look angry.

This was the densest forest near the capital; the trees only stood a few inches from each other once you left the road. He remembered coming here with his mother once, and being scared that the trees would swallow them whole. His mother had told him that the trees cared not for men, for they had lived hundreds of years and had seen men born, live their lives, and die.

"It's a good thing we have you then," he smiled. "You're the only person that can work these angry trees if it's needed"

Emma blushed and looked the other direction. Jason couldn't help but admire how humble she was. He knew that if he'd been born with her abilities, he would have been very different.

An eerie peacefulness hung in the air as they walked in the dim, filtered light. The sounds of their footsteps and the carriage wheels scraping the ground were the only noise that surrounded them. No birds or animals came near the path, many would be born and die in the forest without ever seeing a human.

They walked for hours amongst the winding rows of trees. The carriage barely fit between the branches, and several times the scratching sound of a large branch on the wooden carriage would startle the group.

The end of the forest was ahead of them, the sunlight bounced off the tips of the trees. Beyond these last few feet was another half mile of fields. Then, they'd arrive in Chelmsford, just in time for the King to have dinner with the local Duke.

During their meeting, they'd discuss taxes and military drafts over drinks. Jason knew the King would get whatever he demanded of the Duke. He had no standing army and was too close to the capital to rebel or make threats. This trip was merely meant to make the Duke and his city feel valued.

The people of Chelmsford had been restless the past few months, and demanded recognition of their efforts. After the King's visit, the Duke would give a speech announcing their 'negotiations' and it would strengthen the common people's bonds to the capital. The alliance would continue for the next several years, until another visit would be needed.

Jason had witnessed his father manipulate people his whole life. He had a talent for making them feel valued when all he cared about was their money. When Jason was young, he had asked his father about giving food rations to the refugees that lived along the coastal cities. His father had laughed at the idea, saying that the refugees were better off dead than burdening his people. It was then that Jason started to resent his father, but he never spoke out against him publicly.

The sun shone brightly on them, as if celebrating their departure from the forest. It was comfortably warm and the breeze across the fields felt cool and refreshing. The city of Chelmsford stood like a beacon of tall red brick buildings surrounded by a pale grey wall. The city was beautiful, and almost as large as the capital. The Duke's castle was in the exact center of the city.

King Terril's voice boomed out of the carriage. "How much further?"

Jason rolled his eyes and replied, "We'll be to the city in about fifteen minutes, and then it'll be another hour to the castle."

The King mumbled something through the carriage curtains, but Jason didn't bother asking what his father was complaining about. He was not a very patient man, and spending all day in the carriage had made him more ornery than usual. He'd be glad to part ways once they arrived.

Jason looked over each of his trainees. John still marched with his head held high, his attention focused firmly ahead of them. While he was arrogant, he was a born soldier with a strong sense of discipline. Harper on the other hand seemed to be losing her concentration. She walked with determination, but her vision fluttered from the fields to the walls, to the archers that guarded the city, and then down to the gates. She seemed to be absorbing everything there was to see of this city, but not paying much attention to anything in particular.

Adam ambled with a slower gait than the rest. He seemed less concerned with maintaining formation now that they were near the bustling city. His focus scarcely left John's back; if John moved to the right a few paces, so did Adam. Jason couldn't tell if the mimicry was intentional or not. He also didn't know whether it was out of a kind of admiration or caution. He'd seen them mock each other plenty, but also help each other during training. There was no doubt they were rivals, but he wasn't sure if they were friends as well.

#

The castle doors were made of thick walnut and stretched almost twenty feet in the air. Four guards stood at attention outside the castle. They waited until they saw Jason before they opened the doors to allow them into the courtyard.

Lush green hedges lined the perfectly manicured yard. It smelled of crisply cut roses and fresh rain, and the lawn beneath them was perfectly trimmed. Jason tapped on the door of the carriage as it stopped, and waited for his father's acknowledgement.

With a loud crack, the carriage door swung open and the King barreled out. He rubbed his hips and looked sourly at his son as he stepped out of his seat. He grumbled under his breath that it was 'about damn time' and turned his attention towards one of the guards.

"Why isn't the Duke here to greet me?"

The guard stammered, "A-a-apologies your majesty, he's just inside the dining hall awaiting your arrival. He wanted to ensure your favorite ale was ready for you."

The King grunted and nodded, "Well lead the way then. We've been travelling all damn day."

The guard led him to a nearby door and the two of them disappeared inside. Jason was disgusted at how his father treated those he thought were beneath him, but as King, there was no one that could tell him otherwise.

Jason instructed his trainees to help put away the horses and come to the meeting hall when they were done. A small meal would be placed out for them there, and then they could all get some well deserved rest while his father manipulated the Duke.

Once they were back in the Capital he'd have a chance to tell Emma about their next mission, but for now they could relax. He'd be giving her a new test soon enough.

CHAPTER 11

Two years. Two hard years of training had led up to this day. Her body tensed with anticipation, adrenaline coursed through her. She took deep breaths – in and out, in and out – trying to calm her nerves and clear her mind.

Now was her chance to prove what she'd learned, for everyone to see that she wasn't the shy, meek little girl that entered the Academy two years ago. She would finally be able to show Jason what she was capable of doing. This mission *had* to be a success.

Emma paddled quickly against the icy currents that pushed against her. For every inch she swam forwards, the waves seemed to thrust her two inches back. Ever since she began training, she'd gotten stronger, and she knew if she focused that she would make it soon. In the distance she could see the hull of the boat.

Just a little further.

Focused, she continued to pull the hydrogen out of the water around her, holding it carefully in front of her like a bubble. It was difficult to maintain this movement while kicking and keeping her head above the waves, but this was the fastest way to move against the currents. For this mission, it was critical that she board the boat quickly and without being spotted.

This was her hardest mission yet, one that she had been preparing for for weeks. Emma was in it alone, without Adam. Jason would come in later, but for the most part, she was going solo.

She was tasked with killing the infamous Captain Read, who had been an enemy of the King for years. Jason had told her that he had been intercepting navy ships and stealing their supplies en route to several local outposts. Emma wasn't sure of the details, but she knew he was a threat to the King, and for that, he would have to go.

It wouldn't be easy; Captain Read had specially trained pirates on his ship to guard him. They wouldn't go down without a fight.

The wooden hull floated above the water ahead of her, bouncing up and down in the rough seas. She'd been hoping for better weather, but she didn't have the luxury of waiting. Once she boarded the boat, Jason would only be a few minutes behind her on a boat of his own. She'd have to take out the pirates before then, they'd be watching for ships, but not a lone swimmer. Swimming this distance in the Hever Sea would be suicide for most.

Her hand reached out and brushed the wood. It was smooth and worn down from the constant battering of the sea. She would need to focus all of her efforts into the next few minutes, after which Jason would come to help her finish the job. Everyone aboard the ship was a threat now; hundreds of pirates were aboard, and it was critical that she got to Captain Read.

Now.

Emma focused on the water that brushed against her feet and worked it into a solid grip around her ankles. Satisfied with her control, she pushed it against herself. She shot upwards alongside the boat.

A chilled burst of air hit her face as she jolted out of the water. She breathed in deeply and positioned herself on a pillar of water that stood above the boat. She jumped down onto the deck.

A group of men gazed blankly at her. Their faces were paralyzed with shock. They couldn't believe that a small girl like Emma had just shot out of the sea and landed on their ship.

She looked away, not meeting their eyes or acknowledging them. Not seeing their faces made her job easier.

Emma's head pounded from the crashing of the waves. She wanted to sink into the floor of the boat and just catch her breath for a moment. But, there was no time for recovery; she had to focus and launch her attack.

Emma pushed the water away from herself, turning it to ice and wrapping it around the pirate's ankles. She worked quickly, her palms moving in a repeated sequence. By the time they could react, she had already covered their ankles, hands, and mouths in thick blocks of ice. They were immobilized, but the loud noise would attract more pirates from inside the ship.

The crackling sound of ice filled the air as the men tried to break free of their bonds. Emma hoped they would stay immobile. If they managed to break free, she'd have to kill them.

Emma turned around and faced the large double doors that led into the ship. Another handful of men came rushing out. They were the water elementalists.

Their eyes darted towards the men she had just trapped, then back to her. In a synchronized motion, they shifted into their stance and released them of their ice shackles. Emma swore under her breath.

"Who the hell do you think you are?" A man yelled as he ran at Emma, wielding a short sword.

Emma stood still, waiting for the right time to strike.

The man swung his sword angrily at her stomach, and Emma moved her hand down. The steel fell to the ground in a silvery puddle. The man stepped back in shock.

Emma took the opportunity to pull a large stream of water from the sea to create a ring around her that pushed outwards. The men saw it coming, and pushed back against the water that threatened to heave them overboard. They barely managed to keep their balance.

Emma had not expected the pirates to be this strong. She didn't want to, but she knew that she would have to hurt them to get to Captain Read.

Frustrated, she reached towards the liquefied steel at her feet and pulled it up into the shape of several long, pointed needles. In one quick motion, she shot them through the ring of water towards the men.

Screams of pain filled the deck.

Several men dropped to their knees and clutched their stomachs with their hands. She had hit them strategically below their ribcages, and pierced them through their abdominal muscle wall. It wasn't lethal, but the pain was intense.

Emma turned her body to face the few men left standing. She stretched out her arms and pulled back swiftly, tugging at the elements inside them. The simple movement squeezed their internal organs and pushed the air out of their lungs. It wasn't enough to kill them, but she knew it would cause them incredible pain. The men cried for her to stop as their eyes filled with tears and they crumbled to the floor.

An alarm siren blared on the ship. They knew she was here.

The sound of footsteps rushed towards her, men shouted as they barreled out at her from below deck. They were all armed with swords, ropes, and long kitchen knives.

Emma had to strike quickly.

She grabbed onto the nearby mast to stabilize herself and pulled at the water alongside the boat. She worked a large wave up and over the sides. She forced a wall of water to crash over the men.

Many men slipped and collapsed in a heap on the floor. Some managed to keep their balance, but Emma quickly manipulated the water around them and turned it to ice. The thick ice held the men firmly in place. She was confident that they didn't have any chance of freeing themselves now that the water elementalists were also trapped.

Emma looked around to ensure that all the men left on the deck were either dead, too hurt to move, or trapped. She then jumped down onto the lower deck, careful not to slip on the ice as she weaved between bodies towards the head of the ship. Captain Read would be inside the Captain's quarters at the front, tucked away in times of danger like this. All she had to do now was find – and eliminate him.

Sweat coated her skin, and her hair felt sticky against her neck. It wasn't a hot day, but her heart raced. She was exhausted.

As she made her way to the front of the ship, Emma swallowed. There was a split at the base of the stairs leading under the deck, opening up to two paths. Both were shrouded in darkness with the only light coming from a torch further down each hallway.

Instinctively, she darted right. It was a shot in the dark, but the sooner she moved, the sooner her mission would be done.

A hand grasped her by the shoulder as she began to run. She spun around quickly, prepared to kill whoever was there.

It was Jason.

What is he doing here already?

She couldn't help smiling when she saw him. She wished she had completed the mission before he got here; this was her hardest mission yet, and he would have been impressed by her skills. But at least he had arrived when she was almost done. He had to know that Emma had single handedly defeated the pirates upstairs.

Jason motioned to the left and pointed to himself. Then, he pointed to Emma and gestured to the right. He wanted them to split up. Emma felt a pang of disappointment, wishing they could go together so he could see her in action. Despite her disappointment, she knew that strategically it was better this way.

She nodded and they parted ways. Her heart pounded as she ran down the hallway to the right. Darkness enveloped her as she delved into the belly of the boat. As she approached the end of the right hallway, the echo of Jason's footsteps faded into nothingness. The air was still and she walked quickly. She tried her best to make no sound as the soles of her shoes hit the floor of the deck, remembering something Dominic had said: "If the enemy hears you, you're as dead as if they saw you."

Her eyes adjusted slowly to the low light in the hallway. The lanterns that hung on the walls barely provided enough light to walk by. Everything was quiet.

It was *too* quiet. It didn't feel right.

A sinking feeling washed over her, and something told her Jason was in danger. She looked around; she was alone, and there were no sounds coming from this direction. This side of the ship was empty, meaning all of the remaining men had to be on the other side, where Jason was.

She whipped around and ran down the path where Jason had gone. She couldn't shake the feeling that he was in trouble.

I hope I'm not too late.

Emma bolted down the hallway, no longer caring about stealth or remaining quiet. Her footsteps hit the floor hard, the sound echoing off the walls. Her lungs struggled for air and her eyes strained to watch where she was running in the dim light.

She passed where they had split ways and continued sprinting. Suddenly, she heard a scream.

Jason.

Emma gulped, her instincts had been right.

There he was, a crumpled heap on the floor surrounded by a dozen men. They were laughing cruelly. Their snorts and snickers filled the air. Jason was shaking and gulping for air. His eyes were glassy and his cheeks were red.

Emma stood in shock, trying to catch her breath. *What's happening?*

A man facing away from her kicked Jason hard in the ribs and laughed.

Her blood felt hot as she let out a piercing yell. The men jumped and spun around. They looked at Emma, and as if she wasn't even there, turned back to Jason. One man kicked him again and spit on him.

"Little prince is weak after all," a short man with a long brown beard snorted.

Captain Read.

Emma scowled at him. Jason had warned her that Captain Read was a master in controlling oxygen. He could pull it out of your lungs and suffocate you. Emma was thankful she remembered this; she knew he was killing Jason, and she knew exactly how he was doing it. She could stop him.

Her feet thrust forward and she sent a wave of air towards Captain Read. He looked up.

With a single flick of the wrist he pushed the air to the side, causing the wooden walls of the room to crack and groan. Several paintings and maps fell to the ground. Jason stopped struggling and was now lying motionless on the floor.

All of the men in the room turned and looked at Emma with their dark soulless eyes.

Captain Read took a step towards her.

"Looks like his bitch has come to save him. Too bad you're too late."

Emma glared at him with a hatred she had never felt before. Her world was spinning. In her two years of training, she had never wanted to kill someone. But these men were different. They were genuinely evil.

Three of them stepped closer to her. They weren't elementalists; Emma could sense it. Their hands wrapped around the hilts of their swords. Steel. Carbon and iron, unworkable by anyone.

Except her.

The man nearest to her drew his sword and skillfully thrust it towards her. She dodged to the side of it, waiting for all three of them to brandish their weapons. The second man raised his above his head and brought it down quickly beside her. It grazed her shoulder, just enough to send a bright stream of blood dripping down to her elbow. She grimaced in pain and the men laughed. It burned, but she stood her ground, determined to move only when they had all drawn their swords.

There we go.

The third man's sword was drawn.

Emma focused on the blades as they came at her and dropped low into a squat, her arms facing outwards. The blades melted around her and morphed into a shiny liquid that dripped to the ground like water.

"Shit!" One man said as he stared as his sword's handle.

Everyone gawked at Emma, dazed and unsure how to react. In their moment of confusion, she charged at the nearest man and knocked him onto his back with a loud thud.

She turned, facing Captain Read and two others. Their faces twisted from confusion to rage. With a solid swipe, she used the steel from the swords to form large metal balls, and hurled them towards the men and Captain Read.

She struck them on the side of their heads, knocking two men hard into the wall. Read barely managed to cushion the blow with a pocket of air, but was still forced back a step. His face curled into a vicious snarl.

Jason sputtered; he was still alive.

"NO!" Captain Read yelled, repulsed by the sound of his sputter. His face was crimson and veins protruded sharply from his neck. "NO."

He turned his attention back to Jason, viscously pulling the air away from him.

"He has to die!"

Emma darted towards Read, and in a moment of impulse flung her fist at his jaw. She was so overcome with rage that she couldn't think to do anything else.

Read ducked just in time and let out a snort. The remaining men grabbed at Emma, and pulled her off of Captain Read while he dragged more air out of Jason's lungs. They pulled at her hair and punched her repeatedly. Tears came to her eyes as she tumbled to the ground.

She looked back up at them and realized she held no compassion for their lives. She wanted them dead. She had killed men before, she could do it again. Her thoughts raced to the men she had drowned on her first mission. It had been two years, but their desperate fights to remain alive still haunted her.

The deaths of these men would not cost her sleep.

With a determined pull, she reached into the air towards the men who kicked at her, and felt the carbon inside them. Then, she felt the oxygen, hydrogen, calcium, and all the other elements that made them human. In her hands, they were nothing more than a mixing bowl of elements. She stared down at her fists and tightened until her fingernails dug into the skin of her palms. She broke the chemical bonds inside them, and dismantled them piece by piece until they were no longer recognizable as humans.

Read lasted the longest of the men. He stared at Emma with deep, dark eyes as he fought against her. After several seconds of struggling, he joined his men as a lifeless pile of blood and flesh.

Emma forced herself to move towards Jason's limp body. Her hand rushed to his neck.

He wasn't breathing.

She couldn't feel a pulse.

"No, don't die!" She screamed as she pounded down on his chest.

She pushed hard against his ribs and leaned in and positioned his head like Dominic had taught them. She breathed into his lungs, pressing her lips against his.

She pushed and breathed, pushed and breathed, pushed and breathed.

"LIVE!" She yelled, her shriek was muffled by the lump in her throat.

Tears and snot trickled down from her face as she sobbed, desperately trying to revive him. She pressed her entire weight down on him, trying to beat his heart.

"Please Jason," she begged. "Please don't die."

He coughed.

Emma jumped back as his eyelids fluttered ever so slightly. She cried out in relief and grabbed his shoulders in a tight hug.

He was weak, but he was alive.

CHAPTER 12

"Very impressive Emma," Charles said. "You saved Jason's life. The kingdom is in your debt."

Emma smiled at Charles. It had been a long, hard day, but she was glad that everything was going to be okay.

The King laughed and said, "If the boy needed saving, the kingdom needs a better prince."

Charles frowned at the King's remark.

The King had always been hard on Jason, but had belittled him non-stop since they arrived back at Portishead. Nobody had expected that Captain Read and his pirates would come face to face with Jason; it wasn't anyone's fault, least of all his.

"However!" King Terril said loudly as he drank from his goblet. "Emma did prove herself. I think it's time we start sending her and her partner on their own missions."

"Sir," Charles stuttered. Emma had never heard him speak back to the King. "Isn't that too dangerous for them? Emma and Adam have proven themselves, but they've only trained for two years. She's only sixteen."

The King slammed a hand on the table. He looked up and glared at Charles.

"I will not tolerate an argument, not even from you Charles. I said to give them a damn mission. So do it."

Charles stood at attention and bowed.

"Yes, sir."

As Charles and Emma turned to leave, the door to the throne room slammed open. A tall, thin woman with long blond hair rushed in. She held her long skirts in bunches as she ran towards the King. Her cheeks were stained with tears. She looked panicked.

"Marcell," she cried, her voice was stifled by the sniffling. "Why am I not allowed to see my son?"

She fell to her knees before the throne and looked up at the King. Her deep blue eyes were filled with sadness.

"He was weak, woman," the King said angrily. He stood up and looked down at her. "You'll only baby him!"

"Please!" the woman begged. "He's my son! I need to be with him."

The King kicked her to the ground.

"I said no!"

Emma was shocked. How could the King be so heartless?

She took a small step forward to defend the woman, but Charles placed a hand firmly on her shoulder. Emma looked up at him and saw tears in the corners of his eyes.

He shook his head. There was nothing they could do that would help her.

They walked out of the throne room as the King continued to scream at the Queen. Emma had heard that he was unkind towards his wife, but she had never imagined he would be so openly abusive.

Emma couldn't block the image of the King and Queen out of her mind. She just kept replaying the Queen's face; she was obviously used to his violence, conditioning herself against it instead of fighting back. She felt sick to her stomach as they turned down the crooked hallway that led to the Academy.

"Why did he do that?" Emma asked Charles in a low voice, her throat choked with tears. "I've heard how kind and wonderful the Queen is. Why did he hurt her just because she wanted to see her son?"

Charles sighed.

"The King is not a kind man, Emma," he said calmly. "At least not anymore. He would kill his own family if it would win him more power. His father was a warmonger; he raised Marcell to be like him. Proud, defiant and ready to take out his enemies in battle. But Marcell doesn't have a war to fight right now. He takes his anger out on Queen Elizabeth and Jason. Luckily he doesn't take it out on the baby. At least not yet."

Emma was silent for a long time; only the sound of footsteps echoed down the halls as they walked to the infirmary. Finally, after several minutes, they reached the large gray door that led to the infirmary. Jason was inside, resting from their mission.

"You should go see him," Charles said. "But don't tell him about his mother. It'll only upset him. While you're in there, I'll go make sure she's alright."

He paused and shut his eyes for a moment before opening them again.

"The King should have calmed down by now. He probably sent her to the tower again," his voice trailed off and he stared at the doors in front of them.

He shook himself a little and stood up straighter. His eyes were dull, the color from his face drained. Emma could tell Charles cared deeply for the Queen, and hated seeing her treated this way. Emma wished she could hug him closely and console him, but she knew nothing she did would change the reality of the situation.

Charles walked back the way they had come in silence.

A faint, white light peeked through the crack in the door to the infirmary. Emma had spent too many nights here over the past two years; a broken elbow, cracked ribs, two cases of pneumonia and a few times she had collapsed from overtraining. She pushed the door forward and stepped into the room. A shiver ran down her spine.

Nurse Burleson stood over Jason's bed, holding a clipboard and scribbling notes. Her graying hair covered the sides of her face, and it took a moment before she noticed that Emma had come into the room. She looked up briefly and then looked back at her notes.

"Oh, Emma," she sighed. "It's terrible what happened. So much pain so young, it's not good for a boy."

She reached out and laid her hand on Jason's forehead, half of his face was severely bruised.

She looked at Jason with all the affection that Emma remembered having when she watched over Zak. Her heart ached thinking about him. These past few weeks had been so overwhelming that she hadn't thought of him much, but as he came to mind she missed him dearly. She blinked back tears and looked around the room to distract herself.

"Is his mother going to be able to see him after the King calms down?" Emma asked, pushing thoughts of Zak out of her mind.

The nurse stopped running her fingers through Jason's hair and looked at Emma, sadness in her eyes. The wrinkles around her mouth deepened as she frowned.

"I don't think so. Not this time," Her voice wavered.

"Why is the King such a monster..." Emma's voice dripped with anger.

Nurse Burleson snapped her frail fingers at Emma and said sharply, "Shhhh! If he or his servants hear you saying that, he'll have you thrown in the dungeons...or whipped."

"He couldn't hurt me if he wanted to," Emma replied. She was sick of hearing about how powerful he was, when everyone could see he was a heartless man that didn't deserve to be King.

"You don't know what he's capable of," she said as she looked at Jason, half-dead and unconscious on the table. "He'd kill him himself if it benefitted him."

#

Charles ascended a set of cool marble stairs that twisted upwards into a tower. He carried a tray of grapes, cheese, bread, and water. He tried not to spill them as he climbed. It had only been an hour since he had taken Emma to check on Jason, but his thoughts had been running wild ever since. He kept hearing Elizabeth's cries as the King hit her. He had just walked away as if nothing was happening.

Idiot. You should have done something.

Charles had always cared for the Queen. He'd watched her since the day she arrived. She was beautiful and elegant, a stark contrast against the old, rundown enemy ship. No; with her arrival they were no longer enemies. She was the peace offering of Redholt after a ten-year war, and she was to be the new Queen, the bringer of peace.

The entire capital had gathered along the canals as the boat came in. They'd cheered to see their new Queen standing on the front of the boat. She waved at them and smiled. Her arrival meant more food for the children, and the end of the military draft. Peace had finally come in the form of a beautiful, charismatic new Queen.

Charles had gone with King Marcell to greet her. At first glance, the King proclaimed that she was the most beautiful woman he'd ever seen. He rushed to the boat to welcome her to her new country, and insisted that four servants carry her to the castle. She had politely declined and said she would prefer to walk in her new home and feel the ground under her feet.

King Marcell indulged his soon-to-be bride and gave her whatever she desired for months. They were genuinely happy, and their wedding was a grand feast that took weeks of preparation. Everything seemed good then.

Unfortunately, the happiness did not last long. Less than six months into the marriage, the King grew frustrated with his new wife's charitable nature. She cared deeply for the community around her and hated seeing people suffer. Several times a week, she would visit orphans in the slums with her handmaidens, and bring food from the kitchen. The King viewed the refugees as a burden on society. He wanted to kick them out and build a wall around his cities instead.

Often when Charles was guarding the royal chambers he would hear Elizabeth pleading with her husband, reasoning with him that it would be a waste to throw away the palace's scraps when they could go to the children. King Marcell had quickly lost patience with the insubordination and ordered her to never give out 'his' food again.

A few days after that, Charles had run to the King's chamber after hearing a loud crash. He burst through the doors, thinking that thieves must have snuck in. Instead, he saw the King standing over Elizabeth, her eyes puffy and her nose running as she lay crying on the ground.

"Get the hell out, Charles! This is none of your concern!"

"What are you doing to her? She's your wife!" Charles had replied in defiance.

"This bitch may be my Queen, but she needs to learn her place," He threw a heavy marble bookend at the door where Charles stood, barely missing him. "Get out!"

Charles met Elizabeth's gaze briefly; those eyes which used to shine so bright were filled with fear and helplessness. He turned and walked away, closing the large wooden door as the sound of sobs followed him.

The King caught Elizabeth sneaking food out of the castle again a few weeks later, and as punishment had her locked in the marble tower for three days with no food or water. By the time she was let out, she was frail and ill. She had struggled to walk on her own, and needed to be kept in bed for several days under Nurse Burleson's care.

It made Charles feel guilty thinking about how many times he failed to stand up for the Queen. He kept replaying the moments in his head, thinking about all the things he could have said in the years before Jason was born.

Everyone in the castle had hoped that a healthy son would calm King Marcell's rage and restore peace in the family. This son would be his heir, someone to carry forth their traditions and bring pride to the Terrils.

At first, having a child seemed to temper Marcel. He was careful to never harm the baby, or his wife while Jason was with her. Many talked amongst themselves, saying that the King was a changed man. However, when Jason grew older, the King began to lash out at Elizabeth again. He hurt her whenever she did or said anything he didn't like, often hurling anything in his vicinity – a basket, a lamp, a chair – at her without hesitation.

There were times where Jason would look for his mother, but she would be too injured to see him. It was then that Charles started to overstep his bounds as a guard and help as much as he could.

Many times when Jason cried for his mother Charles would take Jason up in his arms and walk to

Elizabeth with him so that they could see each other. Charles began to help the Queen as her guard too; when the King wasn't nearby, she would play with Jason, and Charles would signal to her whenever the King was returning. If the King caught her spending time with Jason without his permission, he would be furious.

It had been years since the Queen had spoken freely to anyone, knowing that it would anger her husband. But after seeing the kindness and empathy Charles afforded her, she began to open up to him. He remembered their conversations over the years fondly, each of them brilliant and thought provoking.

She was an excellent philosopher, and she had an understanding of human nature that went well beyond most. Well-versed and eloquent, she spoke articulately about her dreams, that one day the King would embrace the refugees as equals and raise them as citizens. Unlike the King, she was practical and prudent. She reasoned that by lifting the prejudice against the refugees, the kingdom would strengthen and in turn, the economy would prosper. With the country united as one, they would finally be able to move past the war.

Charles knew the King would never give in to any plans that involved helping the lower class or the less fortunate; he thought it tarnished his country's image.

Over time, the Queen had come to accept that she was powerless. She gave in to the King's orders and kept her opinions to herself. All she wanted now was the hope that her son could have a better life. She often asked Charles to make sure he was safe when he was outside of the castle. Charles always obliged, and kept an eye on the growing Prince.

Charles shook his head as he reached the top of the tower. His thoughts were clouded with memories as he knocked gently on the door.

"Elly?" He whispered. "I have some food for you."

Gently, he pressed the door open and walked into the dim, dusty room. The walls were made of a thick gray marble that looked damp. A single narrow window let in a faint strip of light.

Queen Elizabeth sat upright in a high chair looking out the window, the blades of her bony shoulders poked through her silk gown.

"Thank you, Charles," She said. "You're too good to me."

She turned slowly towards him, a forced smile on her face. Charles thought to himself how very different it was compared to her early days in Portishead. Back then, the corners of her mouth were always slightly upturned in a grin, her skin glowed and her cheeks were rosy. She looked pale and broken now.

"Will you sit with me a while?" She asked.

Charles hesitated. He knew the King was still angry, but even so, it was not too uncommon for him to send a servant to check on Elizabeth periodically throughout the day. The King was a monster, but somewhere inside he did care about his wife surviving.

If Charles was caught, he'd be stripped of his title and beaten. Possibly killed if the King was feeling angry enough, but he would not leave her alone now.

"Of course I will, my Queen," he said as he looked at her. He cracked half a smile at her, hoping the formality would amuse her.

She laughed softly and looked at him. Her hair dangled elegantly in front of her face; her right eye was bruised with a ring of pale blue and purple. Charles wished he could heal her every time he saw her injured. He bent down and kissed her gently just below the mark. He placed a hand over hers delicately and looked at her with concern.

"Why won't you let me take you back to Redholt?" He asked her. "You'd be safe there. From him, from all of this."

Elizabeth pulled her hand away and looked down at the floor. "You know I can't leave my sons. And besides, he'd find us, track us down, and have us killed for it."

"We'd bring the boys, and I could protect you."

Charles held her jaw delicately in his hands and pulled her to look at him. She looked up at him with deep blue eyes; her time here had aged her, but she was still beautiful. He wanted so badly to take her away from this torture and make her happy again.

Elizabeth looked back at Charles, and shook her head.

"You know it would never work."

She grabbed his hands. Delicately, she kissed him and pulled him towards her. Charles ran his hand down her back and placed it on her waist.

Why does the woman I love have to be married to a monster I can't protect her from?

Her body trembled against his, and he knew she was in pain from earlier. He pulled away from their kiss and lowered her back down on the chair. He pushed the tray of food closer to her.

She smiled and began to eat.

"Jason will be okay," Charles said. "I sent Emma to check on him."

"My poor boy," Elizabeth spoke between bites. "I'm glad he has that young girl to keep him company. She seems a bit plain, but I think she's good for him. Smart, and pretty enough, but not petty like the other girls her age. I wonder if they'll make a match."

Charles couldn't help but laugh.

"I don't know, Elly. Maybe. I think the Prince is too concerned with protecting you to care about girls."

She sighed and set down a grape.

"He needs to live his life for himself and Robert, not for his mother. I have you to protect me, Charles."

"But he doesn't know that. He thinks I do exactly what his father says and resents me for it, I think," Charles kicked at the floor as he spoke. "Then again, it's not like he can really ever know."

"No," Elizabeth said firmly. "You're right to not tell him. We know what danger we're in by being together, and he shouldn't be punished too if someone finds out."

Charles nodded and continued to look over the floor in front of him. He vowed to himself that he would find a way to free her from this prison once and for all, even if it killed him.

CHAPTER 13

Their footsteps echoed against the stone floor as they descended the stairs. They made their way to the laboratory that was tucked under the library. They had been sent to get Jason's medicine from Dominic. Nurse Burleson had given them a long list of things she needed for his treatment.

As they grew close to the bottom of the stairs, the smell of smoke filled their nostrils. A strong chemical scent wafted upwards. During her first few weeks here, Emma had been repulsed by the smell whenever she was at the lab. Now it reminded her of Dominic and the skills she had learned from him. In this lab, non-elementalists used science to manipulate the world around them. To Emma, it was fascinating that people with no powers could still make these wonderful combinations of elements, which were used for medicine, weaponry, and many other things.

Charts with symbols and letters lined the walls, and glass vials and bottles filled with various liquids hung from metal racks. Three young men stood near Dominic, taking notes as he spoke. Emma and Adam listened quietly from the doorway.

"By combining heat, carbon, hydrogen, and oxygen in the correct amounts, we can construct small tablets that will assist with pain relief and decrease swelling."

Dominic tapped his cane delicately on three jars in front of him.

"We can alter the effects of the medication by mixing these three elements in different compositions. This jar contains a basic pain relief tablet, one of the most common drugs we create. This is an antibiotic, used for treating almost all kinds of infections, and if we add nitrogen to this one here, we get a fever-reducer."

Emma listened as he explained how the molecules worked together to form various chemical structures and how their properties contributed to their uses. His lecture continued for another half an hour before he finally noticed Emma and Adam watching him. He jumped slightly, startled to see them there.

"Oh, kids, you scared me!" He said as he stroked his beard. "I didn't realize you were in the room! How long have you been there?"

"A while," Emma laughed. "It was interesting and we didn't want to interrupt."

"Well, I'm glad you're here," he smiled and placed a hand warmly on Adam's shoulder. "It's good for you two to learn as much as you can."

Emma watched as two of the younger boys poured liquids of different colors and consistencies together. To her, it almost looked like they were preparing a recipe using narrow measuring cups.

She'd spent countless hours learning about the chemical properties of elements and how the world was made up of tiny compounds, but she was still intrigued that these non-elementalists could do such amazing things. They could even work carbon with simple tools in this lab.

"We're just here to get some medicine for Nurse Burleson," Adam said.

"Oh, of course!" Dominic walked over to his desk and grabbed an armful of bottles, each filled with liquids or small tablets. As he took them one by one, he rattled off which did what.

"What do these have in them, Dominic?" Emma asked as she peered at the contents through the glass. "Could I make them?"

Dominic laughed and leaned on his desk. His long, thin fingers looked pale against the dark blue cloth as he dabbed his forehead with a silk handkerchief. Emma met his gray eyes with anticipation as he pondered her question.

"With enough training," he said. "You might be able to. Right now, I don't think you're delicate enough. But you're smart, and someday, you will be able to control each element at the molecular level and make these medications yourself. Not now though, it can get quite dangerous if you're not careful."

He pointed at a large black smudge on the wall across the room from them. It covered about a third of the surface. It looked as if a huge fire had started there and been put out after it had smoldered for several minutes.

"See that over there?" He looked at the wall, then back at Emma. "A student of mine was working at their desk, and he accidently blew off his hand by mixing things too quickly. Now he has more patience and is one of my strongest students, but he certainly paid a price for that lesson."

Emma was undeterred by Dominic's story. She was still intrigued by the power of chemistry and was confident that she would never be that unfortunate.

"Can you teach me how to do it someday?" Emma asked. She thought about how useful making medicine on missions could be. She could heal people in the field instead of killing. She doubted it would have helped Jason, but in the future, she could see it being handy.

Dominic nodded. "In a few years, you will have refined your skills enough. When that happens, I can train you to focus on this type of more delicate work."

He pulled at the handkerchief, unfolded, then folded it again.

"For now, I think it's best you get that medicine to the infirmary. You've listened to this old man long enough."

Emma and Adam both nodded and turned to leave the lab. They walked back out the way they had come, but decided to take a short detour through the gardens on their way back. It was an unusually nice day; the sun was out, accompanied by a gentle breeze that came and went.

Adam held the bottles tightly as they headed down the path, careful not to drop them. Next to him, Emma plucked a rose and held it close to her nose. She breathed in the flowery scent and sighed.

"I love this time of year," she said wistfully, looking into the distance. "There weren't many flowers where I was in Campton. Sometimes the ladies carried them in the city, but very few people could afford them."

Adam laughed.

"My father and I used to buy my mother flowers every year for her birthday. I mean, they're pretty and all, but I never thought they were anything special. I suppose we come from very different backgrounds. Are you glad to be off your raft and living here?"

Emma twirled the rose between her fingers and watched the petals catch the breeze.

"I am, but I miss my old life sometimes. Mostly I miss Zak," she said, thinking about what he might be doing now. "I got a report on him a few weeks ago. He bought a house and a beagle named Rex. I wish I could go visit him, or have him come here."

"Maybe once we move up the ranks, they'll invite him here," Adam said. "Plus, if we ever have a mission near Campton, we could just go off book for a few hours and stop by. I'm your partner, so I wouldn't tell."

He smiled at her and winked. She thought about how lucky she was to have him, rather than someone like John, for a partner. But at the same time, she wondered if she'd perform better on missions with Jason. Their most recent one had failed miserably, but it wasn't his fault. Missions could have unpredictable circumstances, and anything could happen.

"I'd like that," Emma said quietly. She let the rose drop to the ground beside her as they continued walking.

She continued to think about Zak, and what he'd think about her as an assassin. Would he understand?

Would he see her as the monster she felt like she was becoming? They continued the rest of the walk in silence as she let her mind wander.

#

The infirmary felt colder than usual as the wind blustered in through the open window. Jason sat upright, his back pressed against the wall and the bottom half of his body under a thick wool blanket. He didn't look at them as they entered the room, but stared through the window with a blank expression. Emma walked up to the edge of the bed and sat down by his feet, she placed her hand on his leg.

"How are you doing?" she asked quietly.

Jason turned to look at her with empty eyes. His voice cracked as he replied. "I shouldn't have taken you on that mission, Emma. It was too dangerous. You could have died."

"I wanted to go on that mission," she replied. "There's no way you could have known it would be so risky, and we both made it out alive, and --"

"There is no 'and'," he cut her off. "I should have insisted on more intel – intelligence –before taking you on that field mission. Charles said at the start that he didn't think you should go, and he was right."

His shoulders slumped forward. His breathing became uneven as he fought back tears.

"It isn't your fault, Jason," Emma said calmly. She was surprised at Jason's sudden display of emotion. Normally he was so composed it was hard to tell what he was feeling.

"It is, though," Adam said from across the room. "He could have gotten you killed, all because he wanted to impress you by going on a mission alone with you."

Emma's face turned red as she spun around, her mouth twisted in a scowl.

"How can you say that? You weren't even there. You have no idea what happened!"

"I know that he wants to impress you," he yelled. "He went behind Charles' back and brought you along. Well, it may not have worked out as planned, but at least now he has your pity."

"I don't want her pity!" Jason screamed hoarsely as he lurched his body forward. "I want her to be safe and I feel horrible that she had to rescue me."

"Good. You should," Adam said. "She's a trainee, just like me. She shouldn't be doing missions like that yet."

"STOP IT!" Emma shrieked. "What is wrong with both of you?"

The boys stared at each other, anger pulsed through the air between them. They continued to glare at each other in silence while Emma paced up and down the room, thinking to herself. After a few moments, she sat back down and breathed in deeply.

"All that matters right now is that Jason is getting better. Adam, I think you should leave. Leave the medicine on the table. I'll let Nurse Burleson know."

"But..." He began to argue.

"No, we can talk later. I want to talk to Jason now."

Adam sulked as he placed the medicine on the wooden side table. He shuffled his feet and turned to the door when a loud blasting sound suddenly shook the walls, kicking dust into the air and making everyone jump. The floor vibrated. They struggled to keep their balance. Another loud blast shook them again. Emma clasped her hands hard over her ears.

"What was that?" She screamed, trying to make sure her voice could be heard above the explosion.

"I don't know," Adam said. He was covered in a thin layer of dust. "It sounded like an explosion near the library."

Emma's heart pounded in her chest. Did something go wrong in the lab? Dominic had just talked about chemistry experiments backfiring and causing explosions. Maybe one of the students had messed up and caused a bad reaction. She panicked, worried about what might have happened. Something told her that she had to go investigate.

She burst into action. Her feet pushed hard against the ground as she ran towards the noise. She could smell the smoke before she turned the corner and saw the fire licking at the wooden arches of the library. The fire sucked up the books greedily, growing off of them as it rushed up the length of the room.

Suddenly, Emma heard a shriek from a corner. *Dominic. No!*

Emma couldn't see him through the smoke, but his screams were loud. He had to be nearby.

She moved around the room, straining her eyes to spot him.

"Dominic!" She shouted. "Where are you?"

His screams continued on and off, echoing with pain. He tried to speak, but his words were muffled.

She could barely hear him, and couldn't make out what he was saying or where it was coming from. She lunged forward, focusing on the air around her trying to clear it so she could see properly.

Damn. No luck.

She turned and tried again. She concentrated and moved her body forcefully.

There.

He was pinned under a bookshelf that had been knocked over by the explosion. She ran towards her screaming mentor. With all her strength, she pushed the shelf upwards and freed his body. She grabbed him and tugged at his arms, pulling him out of the rubble. He clasped his palms around her neck as she carried him out of the library, coughing and sputtering as they moved through the thick smoke.

Masked men stood on the lawn outside. As Emma looked closer, she realized they were throwing flaming bottles at the buildings. The library was engulfed in flames, its outline faint amongst the red and orange embers that sparked in the sky. The men aimed at the west wing of the castle, where the Queen's quarters were.

Emma felt her blood boil as she watched the men bomb the building as if it were nothing. They set the guards on fire as they ran towards them with their swords outstretched.

The masked men had elementalists with them that fueled the fires with air and pushed the flames higher, ensuring that everything they attacked burned to the ground...and took the people with it.

Carefully, Emma laid Dominic down in the grass before running towards the men in black masks. Her hands curled into tight fists, and rage coursed through her with a force that made her shake violently.

I have to stop them.

A nearby man jumped, startled by Emma's sudden presence. He stopped and spun around. His mask stretched above his nose to his eyebrows, but Emma could see his green eyes glaring at her.

"Get out of here, little girl," he yelled. He held a bottle in his hand, prepared to light the soaked rag that stuck out of it.

Emma forced the bottle to explode in his hand as she lit the air inside the bottle. Large shards of glass blew up in front of him, leaving bright lines of blood across his tattered clothes as he fell to the ground. He screamed in pain as Emma stepped over him and continued towards the front lines. She ignored his pleas, she had work to do.

Two more men to her right ran towards her, lobbing their makeshift bombs at her. She shot them out of the air with a blast, manipulating the fire around her to spin and circle around her like a moving shield. She was enraged, and it made her stronger. She would not be stopped by these men; they were nothing to her. They had attacked her home, and they would pay for it.

In a fit of anger, she lurched her body outwards, sending balls of fire towards a dozen men who stood in front of her. The flames ate at their clothing, forcing the men down to the ground in agony. Emma did not look at them, but continued moving forward where another group of masked men stood.

"Get her!" A voice yelled.

Three more men charged in her direction and aimed their flames at her.

She deflected them easily; their power was nothing compared to hers. She had trained with the best for over two years and had grown to be one of the strongest among them.

Instinctively, she pushed the oxygen in the air out in waves, feeding the flames as she manipulated them. She whipped the men around her, enveloping them in a fire that consumed them.

Her mind went blank as she cleared the lawn of the men in masks. She slaughtered them as her anger consumed her. She had only felt rage like this once before, when Jason was dying in front of her.

She lost control of herself and continued to burn down the men around her, hitting a few that were nearby in her wall of fire. It wasn't until she saw the last man on the ground that she stopped, exhausted.

She looked around, her heart beat fast from the adrenaline. Her stomach dropped as her eyes fell on the motionless bodies of five guards she had struck in her rage. They were lying on the ground smoldering, crying out in pain – first loud and piercing, then slowly, they grew quiet.

Her eyes watered and tears flooded down her cheeks. She couldn't believe what had just happened. She buried her head deep in her hands and sobbed.

What have I done?

CHAPTER 14

Emma couldn't stop crying long enough to answer Charles' questions about the attack. Even if she could, there wasn't a point; everything was a blur. She couldn't piece the events together in her mind.

Her head hammered with pain. She was too choked up to speak, and her mind was a whirlwind of thoughts that just kept repeating, one after another.

She remembered the fire and rescuing Dominic. She still felt the panic inside her that she had tried to suppress. There were gaps in her memory, each filled with the cries of people she was hurting and the emptiness she felt as she watched them fall, one by one.

"Emma, you need to calm down." It was Jason, his voice full of concern. "Everything will be okay. You saved a lot of people out there. They never would have made it without you."

She shook her head, her eyes closed shut. There was no way she could justify what she had done. She may have saved some lives, but she killed more than she had saved. They didn't all deserve to die. She had been heartless and cruel, and didn't think about the consequences of her actions. How could Jason look at her after that?

He put an arm around her slumped body, waiting patiently for her sobbing to die down. He placed his palm delicately under her chin and edged it upwards, prompting Emma to look him in the eyes.

"Everyone knows you only did what you had to," he said, his voice was sincere and comforting. "Please talk to us."

Emma shrugged away from him, pulling herself free. She bent her legs and buried her head between her knees. Her cheeks were puffy and she sniffled loudly, hiccupping once every few seconds.

I can't keep doing this.

Everything that had happened in the past few hours brought back memories of all the lives she had ended in training, all the people she killed on missions without a second thought.

I'm a monster.

Charles whispered something to Adam and Jason. They left the room. Charles sat down next to Emma and waited for several minutes before speaking.

"You saved Dominic's life," Charles said, breaking the silence. "Nurse Burleson said he would have suffocated if you hadn't gotten him out. His wounds are still pretty bad, and it'll take time to heal. But he'd be dead for sure if it weren't for you."

Emma held down a cough as she cried. Her chest heaved with every breath.

"You also saved Queen Elizabeth and the baby, Prince Robert," he whispered. "Without you, they would have burned alive. I owe you my life for saving her. You're a hero, even if you don't see it."

Emma wasn't sure how to react. Was she really a hero if she had been the reason for the deaths of innocent guards? She looked up, surprised to see that

Charles was crying. His eyes were swollen slightly and his cheeks looked red.

"You love her, don't you?" Emma asked.

Charles looked at her with pain in his eyes, and said, "She is my Queen. I will serve her until the day I die."

It was clear to her that it killed him to watch the King torment her. Emma wondered if the queen knew how he felt.

"I feel like a monster," she confessed. "Like something that should be caged up and locked away, not praised for hurting and killing people on command."

"It's our duty to serve our King," Charles said. "It can consume us, but we give up ourselves to protect those we love. To ensure their happiness, we make sacrifices so others don't have to."

Emma sat upright and reached her hand into her left breast pocket. She pulled out a piece of paper and carefully unfolded it. It was a sketch of her brother, drawn by one of the guards who had last checked in on him. She'd received it as a reward after a successful mission a few months ago. It hadn't left her side since. It reminded her of why she was doing this; because it meant that he was happy and safe.

"I don't want to be a killer," she said in a low voice. "But I want him to have a good life."

"I'm so sorry, Emma," Charles said. "I found you and brought you to the King, knowing you would do anything for your brother. I knew how he'd use you. It's my fault."

Charles stood up and began to pace. Emma wanted to tell him she was glad he'd come to her, that at least her brother was happier, but he began to speak before she could.

"The King wants to send you on another mission. This is an important one, and if it's successful, it will ensure that the rebels never attack us in the city again."

Emma nodded. She knew she wouldn't like this mission.

"He wants you to go undercover as a rebel and kill their leader. If you're able to do that, he's agreed to let you go on tour with me for the next two years. I won't make you fight or go on missions. I plan for you to study alongside me, to learn about the history and politics of the Kingdom. People come here and think it's all about the fighting and the action, but they're wrong. We value knowledge very highly, and I want you to see that."

Emma swallowed.

She dreaded the thought of killing the rebel leader, but she knew that the King wouldn't take no for answer. Besides, just studying for two years was definitely preferable to going on more missions and being responsible for ending more innocent lives. She had had it with all this violence.

"How does that sound, Emma?" Charles asked.

"I'll do it. If I can see Zak."

Charles thought for a moment and then nodded.

"I think that's a fair trade. I'll figure out how to sneak us both there once you're back."

#

"When it's all over, she sees the wreckage she's left behind, the destruction she's responsible for. She's miserable. How can you send her out there alone? Especially now, after all that's happened," Adam said.

"I don't have a choice," Charles said flatly.

His face was stern and his eyes stared past Adam into nothingness. His gaze was empty.

"The King gave me orders, and I discussed the mission with Emma. She agreed to the terms almost immediately. There's nothing I can do."

"Of course there's something we can do," Adam shouted. "I can go with her. She needs someone to watch her --"

"No," Charles interrupted. "It won't work if she has a partner. The rebels will never believe the cover for two people. They'll be suspecting backlash from the King, and they'll be too cautious for our plan to work."

"At least let me shadow her," Adam said desperately. He couldn't bear the thought of her out there, all alone. "Meet with her and check in on her regularly. I just want her to be safe."

His lips quivered as he spoke. He had grown fond of Emma over their time as partners, he was always impressed by her strength and determination. The last thing he wanted was for her to be in danger. Conducting this last kill, after her breakdown earlier, was bound to affect her and send her on a downward spiral.

Charles looked at Adam. His forehead was creased with worry and his eyes were sullen.

"I know how you feel about her, Adam, and how much you care for her. It's been obvious since you first carried her back from the mission with Pon. But you can't protect her from this. Trust me, I care for her safety as much as you do, but you'll have to sit this one out. I'm sorry."

Adam nodded in defeat as he turned to leave the room. Part of him knew that if he was there, Emma would be too distracted to focus on the mission. Maybe it was for the best.

Charles stared into the crackling fireplace while the mellow flames cast a warm glow around the room. His eyes followed the movement of the dancing embers as he thought about all the children he had mentored through the years. Many of them felt like his own. They were a part of him; he took pride in their achievements, and when they got hurt, he suffered with them. He dreaded walking down to meet Emma in the courtyard to break the bad news, but he knew it had to be done.

With a deep sigh, Charles walked out of the room, his gait heavy and slow. He closed the wooden door behind him softly.

The hallways were chilly, and Charles pulled his jacket up snug against his neck. His pace quickened as he got closer to the courtyard, his heart pounded in his chest.

As he turned the corner, he stopped.

Emma sat on a bench under a small cherry tree and fiddled with a small branch. Charles watched as she twirled it slowly between her fingers. Her eyes looked off in the distance, not focused on anything in particular. The way her brows were furrowed, she was obviously deep in thought. Her face sank in a slight frown, and her cheeks were puffy from crying.

Charles moved to sit silently beside her.

"Emma," he said quietly as he rested a hand gently on her shoulder. "How are you doing?"

Emma didn't react for a moment, as if she hadn't heard him. Eventually she shrugged as she snapped the branch in two. She laid the pieces down on the bench. Her gaze remained listless and unfocused.

"I have some bad news Emma --" he began. His voice faltered.

"Dominic died. You don't have to tell me. I already know."

Charles stopped and looked at her. How had she found out? Only he, Nurse Burleson, and the King knew about his death. He had insisted on giving her the news himself.

"Who told you?"

Emma sniffled, "No one told me. I felt it."

She cried quietly to herself as she spoke.

"Ever since I drowned those men on my first mission, something inside me changed. It's hard to explain, but I've been able to feel when people die. I don't notice everyone, but people that I've become close to, I can tell when their heart stops beating if they're nearby. It's terrifying. When I get that feeling, the air around me seems to surge, I get these little tremors that I can't control. It's like their elements, their bodies, are screaming out to me. They're no longer tied to anything, and it's as if they are willing me to come and put them to use."

That's not possible...is it?

Silence hung between them while Charles processed what she was saying.

He had never heard of any carbon elementalists with such a heightened sensitivity. He knew of elementalists that could sense storms and people that could sense certain minerals around them, but to perceive human life this way was unheard of. It must have been terrifying for this young girl to go through this and to continue on with these missions, each death causing her a physical and mental reaction stronger than the previous. She had been so strong, battling all these emotions, and he had had no idea.

"Emma," Charles stammered. "I'm so sorry. I didn't realize."

Emma looked up at him, her eyes red and teary.

"I know. It's not your fault."

"How did you know it was Dominic?" Charles asked.

Emma thought for a moment before answering.

"Each person has an imprint, I guess because their elemental structures are all a little different from each other. Somehow, I've learnt to subconsciously recognize people by these minor differences. Today, I knew it was Dominic."

Charles pulled Emma into a tight hug, and pressed her head against his chest. He wanted to turn back time and let her return back to her raft, back to her brother. It was all because of him that she was here now. He should have let her run away.

"It'll be okay," Emma pulled away and held herself awkwardly. "I just have one more mission."

Charles watched her walk away in silence; she walked like a weary soldier, not the little girl he had brought here.

#

The city center was bustling as usual, people pressed against each other shoulder to shoulder as they tried to squeeze past each other. Angry conversations filled the afternoon air, a loud buzzing amongst the hundreds of people. A young man, no more than sixteen, stood on a crate and screamed over the crowd. The sweat on his face glistened in the hot sun that beat down on them.

"Brothers! Sisters!" He yelled, cupping his palms around his mouth and waiting for attention. The crowd's murmurs grew to a dull roar as people began to listen. "I know you're angry. For too many years, the royal family has looked down upon us! Well, this ends now! We will rise up against them and show them we cannot be ignored!"

The crowd cheered and whistled their approval. Emma tried to mix in with the crowd, but she felt awkward and out of place screaming obscenities about the king.

The boy continued to yell to the crowd, riling them up for a riot. More people started filing in to surround him, their heads tilted up. Their eyes burned with anger as they watched the boy speak with confidence and conviction.

Just remember the plan. The guards will be here soon.

The crowd quickly became restless. It was on the verge of riot.

"Screw the king!" A man yelled.

"Burn the palace," a woman cried. "Burn them down."

Emma hadn't expected people to react so strongly; these everyday folk held a strong vengeance against the King. Soon people were yelling over each other and chanting in unison.

"Down with the King!"

Emma joined too in an attempt to blend in.

This feels wrong. I don't belong here.

Suddenly, the discordance of iron clanging against iron rang in the air, drawing everyone's attention to the guards. They marched into position and attempted to funnel the crowd into a narrow space. Their iron swords were manipulated into makeshift gates as they pushed the protesters back. At least a dozen guards circled the city square.

People screamed and hurled rocks at the oncoming guards. The air seemed to burn with hatred. Emma yelled too, shouting insults that she had heard earlier about the King. She recognized many of the guards' faces as they approached the crowd. They knew she was there and that she'd have to defeat them in order for her mission to begin. They were some of the most elite guards, the King's most trusted few, tasked to help Emma gain the rebel's trust.

As the guards shoved the people towards the buildings lining the courtyard, violence erupted. An iron elementalist from the crowd fought with a nearby guard for control of the sword he wielded.

The young boy who had been talking to the crowd shot bursts of air towards the guards. He knocked one off balance.

With swift, successive motions, Emma made the air around her reverberate, causing an ear piercing noise.

Immediately, everyone clasped their hands firmly over their ears. Their faces twisted as they cringed.

Emma's body moved from left to right, pushing huge gusts along either side of her and knocking the guards over forcefully.

It only took a few moments before people began cheering her on. All eyes were on her as she manipulated the whirlwind, taking the guards down one by one. Her heart beat fast as she lifted the iron swords away from the guards and let the wind carry them up to the rooftops.

The whirlwind devastated everything in its path. The guards fell to the ground, groaning in mostly feigned agony as they clutched their ribs and legs. Their wounds were minor, as Emma had been careful not to harm them. She just had to make it look real.

Her heart raced as she looked around her. Dozens of people stared at her, slack jawed as they stood in silence. There she was, a girl they had never seen before, taking on all the guards without batting an eye.

Emma felt anxious as she waited for the young rebel to react.

After a few moments of uncomfortable quiet, he walked towards her with his hand outstretched.

He grasped her hand tightly in his and thrust it into the air while shouting, "This girl will fight for our cause! She is for the people!"

A pause lingered over the crowd before everyone erupted into cheers alongside him.

Emma looked at all the lit up faces, every single one of them looked at her with admiration. People had never cheered for her like this before.

CHAPTER 15

"I'm Warren," the young man from the protest said as he thrust out his hand at Emma. She shook it gingerly and forced a small smile. "What's your name?"

"Emma," she said, her voice cracked slightly.

Her throat felt parched and raw. It took most of her energy to keep from shaking. She was nervous that the plan wouldn't work.

"Well, Emma," Warren said. "I don't know where you came from, but it's a miracle you showed up. Those guards would have whooped us otherwise. We're not the smartest or the strongest of the rebels, but I like to think we're the bravest."

He smirked and leaned back against the side of the cart they rode in. His feet were perched up on a hay bale as they bounced down a narrow trail out of the city. The other four rebels slept nearby, curled up in the back of the cart next to them.

"Just lucky timing, I suppose," Emma said.

Her voice quivered and she hoped Warren hadn't noticed. She stared out at the open fields in the distance and watched how the wind pushed the tops of the wheat back and forth, like a sea of gold that stretched miles in every direction.

"Where are we going?"

"Don't worry about the specifics," he said. "We'll have to blindfold you soon anyway once we get closer.

Our boss doesn't trust just anybody to know our hideout. You have to prove yourself first."

"Didn't I do that earlier?"

Emma raised an eyebrow at him.

Warren laughed again, loud enough to rouse the girl that slept next to him. She threw a small stone at him and rolled over to go back to sleep.

"You were impressive, but that doesn't mean we trust you," he paused to look at her. Emma could feel herself blushing as his gaze lingered. "We'll see what Qwen thinks of you when we get back to base. I'm sure she'll have some questions."

What will Qwen think of me?

Emma imagined herself standing in front of Qwen, her heart racing as she awaited her fate. What would she do if they realized she was a plant from the King? Would they try to kill her outright, or slit her throat while she was sleeping?

Emma swallowed hard. The thought made her nauseous and dizzy. She supposed it would be a fitting end for her if she was caught and murdered, since her mission was to find their captain and kill him.

"How much longer until we're there?" Emma said quietly, trying to distract herself.

Warren scanned the area around them. There had only been farm fields for ages. Emma didn't know how he could have any point of reference, but the pensive look in his eyes made it seem like he was calculating how close they were.

"We're probably 10 or 15 minutes away now."

He nodded to himself.

"I suppose it's about time I blindfold you, actually."

He groaned a little as he stood up and stretched his arms out dramatically as if he'd been sitting for days rather than just a couple hours.

"Do you have to?" Emma asked.

She dreaded being blindfolded. How was she going to keep a lookout for danger if she couldn't see? She would be vulnerable and if they knew her real reason for being here, she was in trouble.

Warren chuckled as he pulled out a small piece of cloth from his back pocket.

"Qwen would have my head if I brought a newbie in without blindfolding them first."

Emma nodded and shifted her eyes down to the hay near her feet.

The floor of the cart creaked loudly as Warren stepped towards her, his fingers gripped the sides of the blindfold. Emma's heart beat nervously. She wished she was anywhere but here. The hairs on her bare arms and legs stood up on end. She hoped Warren wouldn't notice her shaking. She thought about Zak to try and calm herself.

Within a few seconds, Warren had placed the cloth over her eyes and pulled back her hair neatly. His hands were coarse, but he tied the blindfold delicately.

"We were all blindfolded, just like you," Warren said just above a whisper. "I know it's terrifying, but don't worry. You'll probably survive Qwen's interrogation."

Emma gulped.

She could die today, and Warren knew it.

#

Sweat beaded up along the edges of the blindfold. Her palms were clammy and her muscles twitched every few seconds. Her breathing seemed to get louder and louder as she thought about when the cart would pull to a stop.

"We're here."

Emma gulped nervously. She had no idea where she was or what would happen next.

"Does that mean the blindfold can come off?" She asked, fully aware of how much her voice was shaking.

"Soon," Warren said. "Qwen is walking over. She'll take you for interrogation."

Interrogation.

Emma's heart thumped.

Is this the end?

"So, this is the new recruit?" A female voice said.

"Yes, this is Emma," Warren replied. "She saved our tails earlier, so I figured she could be of use."

"Well, I'll determine that." Her voice was slightly louder as she said, "Let's go."

Emma felt a pull on her blindfold, and without warning, it was tugged off in a quick motion. She looked around her; they were in what looked like a cave with a huge fire burning in the center.

Everything looked blurry for a few moments as Emma's eyes adjusted to the light. In front of her stood a girl who was only a few years older than she was. She was slightly taller, with long blonde hair pulled into a tight braid that ran down her back. Her face had sharp features and large, deep blue eyes. She wore a stern impression, but Emma imagined she would be pretty if she smiled.

"This way."

The girl turned and walked along the edge of the cave away from the cart. Emma followed, trying not to trip as she struggled to keep pace with her stride. Qwen was obviously in a hurry.

They walked out of view of the cart and the other rebels that sat near the fire, and turned into a small makeshift room. There were two chairs around a square table carved out of a wooden plank. The girl motioned for Emma to sit down opposite of her, and then proceeded to stare at her in silence, as if mentally taking notes.

"I'm Qwen." She said finally, breaking the silence between them. "No one joins our group without my say. So, obviously, I have some questions."

Emma nodded and swallowed nervously.

Everything – all the careful plans that had led her here – could fall apart right here, right now. She held her breath, anxious to hear what she would say.

"Where are you from?"

"I've lived in Portishead for three years. Before that, I was a refugee in Campton."

"What were you doing in Portishead?" Qwen raised an eyebrow. "Few refugees are able to make it in the big city."

"I'm a thief," Emma said. "But I've been trying to become a merchant."

"How did you make it as a thief?" Qwen asked, her voice was flat and lacked emotion.

"I stole silver. It's one of the elements I can work."

"Interesting," Qwen said slowly. She dragged out each syllable. Emma could feel herself sweating nervously again. "It's just a bit too convenient that you happened to be at the protest to save my guys. That, and the guards went down easily for you. Do you really expect me to believe that a scrawny little thing like you could take down a dozen guards?"

"I guess, yeah." Emma's voice cracked.

Qwen leaned back in her chair. She pursed her lips and looked Emma over again, this time from head to toe.

She sighed.

"I don't know if I believe you. We'll have to test your abilities." She paused for a minute. "For now, go get some food. If I have to kill you, you may as well have a good last meal first."

#

The fire flickered wildly as the boys added more wood to the pile. The embers burned against the darkness of the cave. The warm light danced across the faces of the rebels. Emma hoped they'd soon be her new allies, her mission depended on it.

"Do you want some?" Anna asked, her smile sparkling in the golden glow as she held up a dark red bottle.

"Sure, I suppose so." Emma held out her glass and smiled in return. "Thanks."

"One of the perks of this life," Anna said. "We may risk our lives during our missions, but at least we're fed well. We never go hungry, and Qwen keeps everything running smoothly around here. She's a bit like our mother in a lot of ways."

"What's her story anyway?" Emma asked. "How did she get to be in charge? She doesn't look that much older than me."

Warren laughed and dripped a little wine down the front of his shirt.

"She's basically a badass," He said. "She teamed up with the Captain of the rebellion two years ago, right after he funded the first few missions. Within months, there were too many new recruits to have in one place, so she started this branch here near Alsager. She's basically our second Captain."

That makes sense. I wonder if the king knows this. With different branches that work under separate leaders, operations could be much more efficient. That might make the King's plan to take out the head of the rebellion less effective. Once I kill the Captain, I wonder if King Terril will make me kill Qwen too.

Anna's giggles broke Emma's thoughts as she pointed at two boys that danced around the fire. They were obviously drunk and making fools of themselves.

"So, Emma, where were you a refugee before the capital?" Warren asked while dabbing at the wine on his shirt.

"Campton. I lived out on the rafts near the city."

"Oh, a few of the Baldock Marsh rebels are from Campton!" Anna said excitedly. "They're some of our best fighters too. How did you make it there? I hear that city wasn't exactly refugee-friendly."

"I mostly worked on a fishing boat." Emma shrugged. "I stole when I had to, but for the most part I just worked a lot from a young age."

"Was it just you?" Anna asked.

Emma thought about Zak again and the sacrifices she had made so that he could still have a childhood. She thought of the way his eyes lit up whenever she came home with a treat or brought him into the city. He was easily pleased by little trinkets and never asked for more than they could afford.

"Just me." Emma sighed and ate a piece of cheese off her plate. "What about you two? What's your story?"

Warren stood up straighter and said, "I was a fighter before the rebels. Got into a lot of brawls."

Anna scoffed and smacked Warren on the shoulder.

"Liar. You sold candles on the streets until I brought you here with me."

Warren shrugged. "It's basically the same thing."

"Anyways, we were both living in Auchenbrack by the coast, not too far from Campton. We were pretty lucky that the people there didn't build a wall to keep us out, so we lived in the streets downtown. Warren sold candles while I watched the rich folks' kids when their parents went out. I was always good with children. They liked that I could make little whirlwinds and blow their toys around."

Anna demonstrated by making a small vortex of air. It picked up a few stones and twigs off the ground and she formed the debris into a miniature doll and moved it around. She pushed the air delicately around each piece, moving it deftly like a puppet. Her dexterity and control was amazing.

Warren rolled his eyes and stood up, moving a few steps closer to the fire. He grabbed a flask of water from a nearby stump and returned to sit next to them. Slowly, he poured a few drops into his hands and began to make the water bubble. He tried to make a shape like the doll, but it looked more like a deformed blob. Compared to Anna, his movements were choppy.

Anna laughed, "Sorry Warren, you're just not dexterous enough."

Warren sighed and directed the water back into the flask before taking a drink.

"Well, we can't all be as good as you, Anna."

"What about you Emma? We saw that you can move air at the protest. Can you do anything else?" Anna asked.

Emma thought about all the training she had undergone and the elements she could manipulate. She knew she had abilities that most didn't, but she couldn't reveal them all without appearing suspicious.

"Um, I can work iron, oxygen, hydrogen, silver, and copper a little. So water and air, and some metals, I suppose." Emma took a big bite of her bread as an excuse to stop talking.

"You seem to have a pretty good grasp of moving air at least. You knocked like a dozen people over!" Warren smiled widely. He obviously appreciated brute force more than restraint.

"I guess so," Emma said.

"So, you think you're pretty good, huh?" Qwen said.

One hand rested on her hip as she stood behind them. Emma jumped, not realizing that she had walked up to them while they were talking. The light from the fire cast a shadow over her face, making her features difficult to read.

"She was great, Qwen!" Warren blurted out. "She made a tornado, and the guards were absolutely stunned. They had no idea what was happening. She could have taken out an army. Actually, she could probably even beat you!"

He laughed and took another gulp of wine.

Emma wanted to slink into the shadows. She didn't like being the center of attention, especially when she was supposed to be blending in and keeping a low profile. Plus, she knew that Qwen already doubted her story.

"Well, doesn't *that* sound exciting!" Qwen mocked. She rolled her eyes. "Let's test her now then."

Everyone fell silent, shocked at Qwen's sudden hostility. All eyes turned to Emma, and she felt the stares drill into her. She could feel the heat of the fire more intensely now, like it would rise up and swallow her whole.

"I'll enjoy this one," Qwen laughed. "Come on, stand up. It's time for us to see if you're *actually* what you claim to be."

#

Emma shifted her weight from one foot to another while Qwen addressed the rebels around them. She stood in the center of their circle next to the fire. The test would be in front of everyone. This was the most critical part of her mission; being accepted and gaining their trust.

"It's time," Qwen said. "Let's see how exaggerated this strength of yours is."

Slow, scattered clapping and hoots of encouragement came from the sidelines as Qwen bowed in to their duel. Emma bowed as well, and braced herself for whatever came next.

It only took a few seconds before Qwen struck. With a quick flick of her wrist, she sent a dense cloud of smoke from the nearby fire towards Emma to blind her.

Qwen worked fast, but so did Emma. She saw the cloud coming her way and moved quickly, thrusting away the smoke and dissipating it into the air around them.

As Emma focused on manipulating the smoke, Qwen controlled the oxygen in the air and sent several small balls of rapidly spinning debris in Emma's direction. The stones that were encased in the balls of air cut into her skin, striking her hard. Blood dripped down her arm where one of the stones had sliced her, and she tried her best to ignore the burn.

She's stronger than I thought. Time to try something else.

Emma's eyes darted to the fire near them. With a quick, deliberate motion, she ran a gust of wind through the fire, carrying the flames in a large wave towards Qwen. The wall of fire engulfed her, but Qwen created a small pocket of air around her body to protect herself. She was completely unburnt. The look in her eyes was unchanged.

Frustrated, Emma released the flames and created a whirlwind like she had at the protest. All her frustrations from the day went into building a huge spinning vortex of air that lifted Emma off the ground with it. She started grabbing at the flames and the sticks and stones around her to form a tornado of fire and debris that was several feet tall.

In a rush of anger, Emma propelled the winds towards Qwen.

Qwen raised an eyebrow and without moving her feet, she pushed her right wrist outwards to gain control of the wind. She unravelled the tornado that lifted Emma off the ground, and sent her tumbling.

Qwen stepped over her and used the air as an extension of her hand to choke Emma and hold her down firmly. Emma's heart raced. She knew that Qwen could kill her if she wanted to, unless she revealed her full strength. Her mission would be a failure, they'd know her secret.

She couldn't do it. She had to lie here, defeated, and allow Qwen to pull the wind out of her lungs.

Things went black and fuzzy. She felt consciousness waning; she needed to breathe.

Her chest throbbed and she could no longer see. She couldn't let Qwen kill her. She had to act, mission or not.

"I'm impressed," Qwen said.

She released her grip on Emma just as she was about to strike back.

"You're in...for now."

Emma gasped for breath and gulped in air as quickly as her lungs would let her. A wave of relief washed over her as she regained her senses. She couldn't believe it: she had managed to do it. She was a rebel.

CHAPTER 16

"Don't take it personally," Anna said calmly as she wiped the blood away from Emma's cheeks. It had caked hard on her skin and formed a dry, crusty layer. Her flesh felt raw as Anna rubbed it clean with a washcloth. "She beats everyone. She beat me, and she beat Warren. You held out longer than most, and she didn't kill you. Consider that a win."

Emma nodded and tried to force a smile. Her body ached and her head pounded. She couldn't seem to focus as she looked around the small bunkroom. Emma couldn't remember exactly how they got there. As she scanned the room, she noticed there wasn't much except a few beds, a desk, and several oil lamps hanging on the dark gray walls.

Emma and Anna sat on the edge of the bed that would now be Emma's. It was a small bed, something a child might sleep on, but Emma figured she'd fit if she curled up a bit. Each bed had a thick wool blanket tossed neatly across it. The cave was a little chilly, but not enough to merit such a thick blanket. Emma wondered if the temperature dropped at night after the huge fire was put out. Either way, it was nicer than what she and Zak had had in Campton.

Emma thought back to the raft that they had shared and how they had barely been able to survive the cold of the bitter sea winds. Every night they made it through was a victory. They had one blanket that they shared, snuggled up together against the cold.

One night Zak had gotten so cold that Emma worried he'd never wake up. His cheeks were icy to the touch, his body was motionless. She remembered panicking that he was barely breathing, and decided that a fire might keep him alive.

She took everything she could spare that was flammable: her shoes, a journal, and the extra sweater she had found a few weeks ago and used them to make a small fire on the raft.

It was one of her first times working with fire, and she almost burned their tent in the process.

It was a long, miserable night as she tended to the small fire and watched over Zak. In the morning he finally woke up. He was cold and ill, but he was alive.

"Hey, so..." Anna said. "Do you want to come with on a mission tomorrow?"

Emma snapped out of her thoughts and looked at Anna blankly. Her body ached horribly. She wasn't even sure she'd be able to walk tomorrow, let alone go on a mission.

"Warren and I are going," Anna said as she rinsed the washcloth in a small basin of water. "We're getting food for the refugees of Alsager. There'll be a royal caravan passing nearby, and it should be a simple mission. It won't take long. Good for your first time, plus you'll get to see some of the people we help."

"I'm not sure if I'll be able to," Emma said quietly, glancing at her bruised arms and legs. Just moving her neck caused her to wince.

"Well, if you're up for it," Anna said. "Warren and I could really use the extra help. I'm not that strong, and he's not very good at following plans. The last mission we did like this...well...he almost got us captured."

Emma frowned. She didn't want to go, but she knew she had to if she wanted to secure her place here.

"I'll go."

Anna's face lit up in a smile immediately, her blue eyes glistened in the dim light.

"Thank you!" She grabbed Emma into a tight hug, causing her to yelp.

Tomorrow was going to be a long, painful day.

#

The morning felt peaceful and quiet, with just the sound of the lantern's flame crackling nearby. Emma laid in bed, enjoying the stillness and wondering what her friends were doing back at the Capital. She wondered if Adam was going crazy yet with her gone on a solo mission, and if Jason was finally recovered. She remembered him lying on the boat near death. It was something she'd never be able to forget. Her heart ached at the thought of how close he'd been to dying.

Her body screamed in protest as she tried to roll over. Every muscle ached as she contemplated how she was even going to get out of bed. She was dreading this mission, but she knew she had to help Anna and Warren.

Without a second thought, Emma pushed herself upright and cracked her back as she stretched out. The pain shook her spine as she twisted. Part of her wished that Qwen had just killed her.

"Oh, you're awake! Perfect," Anna sat upright in the bed behind her.

Emma slowly turned her body around, unable to twist just her neck.

"How are you feeling?"

Emma groaned, her back let out another loud pop.

"Well, luckily for you this mission shouldn't take too long!"

Anna had a way of being overly optimistic, something that Emma wasn't used to.

"When do we leave?" Emma asked, her voice was hoarse. "I just want to get this over with."

Anna giggled.

"In about 20 minutes. I set some clothes out for you next to your bed. You were out cold last night. I wish I could sleep like that."

A pair of plain black pants and a tight gray shirt sat at the foot of her bed. She put them on along with a pair of thick socks and boots that Anna handed her. Surprisingly, she felt a bit better after moving around.

After she was ready they walked back into the main area and met up with Warren to eat a quick breakfast of eggs and oatmeal. It was quiet; most of the rebels were still in bed. Emma wished she was too.

#

The streets of Alsager were packed with people, the sound of their conversations flooded the city in a chorus of voices and shouts. The street was covered in filth and garbage, and many of the windows were broken or boarded up.

Emma couldn't remember seeing anything this destitute in Camden, but she reminded herself that not every coastal town had built a wall to keep the refugees out. Here, they had allowed them to live among the people. A power struggle had ensued and guards began breaking into homes to antagonize the people that let refugees live with them. It had been chaos for years.

Emma cringed as she watched an armed guard step over a refugee child that had just tripped. He ignored her cries of pain. Emma rushed over to the child and helped her stand up. Her knee was scraped and bleeding but she wasn't seriously injured.

"It's okay. You'll be fine," Emma said sweetly before slipping the girl a copper coin. "Go get a treat."

The little girl smiled cautiously. Her cheeks were dirty with streaks of mud and tears. She gripped the coin tightly and ran off into the crowd.

"You fool," the guard said. His hand rested firmly on his sword, an evil glint in his eye. "The stupid girl didn't need your pity. You're not from around here, are you?"

"No, I come from a place where we treat humans with respect. You've probably never heard of it." Emma glared at him.

The cheekiness in her voice surprised even Emma. She was usually quiet and reserved, but this guard had pushed her to the edge. She stood up and stared at him. His brow furrowed and he gripped the edge of his sword tighter.

"Listen, girl. I don't care where you're from, but speaking to a guard like that here can, and will, get you killed," his voice was deep and threatening.

Emma's blood boiled.

"I'd like to see you try."

The guard began to pull his sword out of the sheath, but Emma had already manipulated the steel of the blade so it couldn't slide out. The guard struggled to pull out the sword, but it wouldn't budge.

"How will you kill me when you can't even pull out your sword?" Emma laughed and walked back to Anna and Warren. They watched cautiously from across the alley.

The guard screamed at her that this wasn't over and inspected his sword angrily, trying to figure out why it was stuck. Emma just laughed and walked towards the others. She was still feeling sore and didn't feel like fighting before they'd gotten to the caravan, but speaking her mind for once had felt good.

They pushed their way through the crowds and made their way towards where the caravan would be.

"Has Alsager always been this bad for refugees? I thought without a wall that it might be a little nicer than Campton." Emma said.

"Oh no, a few years ago it was peaceful, but recently the guards haven't had any repercussions for torturing the locals for 'protection fees'. It's become a city of crime, where the poor are belittled for no reason." Warren said solemnly.

"Campton is the same now," Anna said wearily. "All the coastal cities are, really. People stopped caring about the refugees, especially anyone that was being paid by the King. He wants the refugees to be so miserable here that they either die or leave. The problem is there isn't anywhere else to go that isn't across an ocean or over a mountain."

Emma couldn't believe that things had actually managed to get worse. She remembered being terrified of the guards in Campton, but she'd never had to worry about being killed unless she was caught stealing. They usually left her alone as long as she stayed out of the way. Here it seemed like they were actively trying to make refugees miserable.

How has it gotten this much worse?

Her thoughts wandered to Zak. How was he doing in this change? It had been months since Charles had gotten a report on how he was. When she'd first gone to Portishead, Charles would give her a report on her brother every few weeks, but gradually they'd grown less frequent. This year, she'd only gotten three updates, and none of them were written by Zak.

Emma worried that the updates might have been fabricated now that she knew what terrible things had been happening outside the Capital. She had to find a way to see him while working with the rebels. If she found him, she'd run away with him.

"Here's the crossing point," Anna said, her footsteps came to a halt. "The caravan should pass by any minute now."

Warren nodded.

"We just need to take out the guards that are escorting it, and then we'll be able to drive the food to a nearby meeting point. We have a friend that runs a meat market in town. If we take him the food, he'll distribute it to the poor as they come in. That's our system we've been using to distribute goods without the guards catching on. So far we've gotten ten caravans worth of food out to the poor."

"Oh!" Anna whispered. "They're early. Get ready!"

They crouched down behind a few boxes that were stacked up along the side of the road. There were six guards walking with the transport. They were alert, aware that an ambush was likely.

Emma's heart pounded harder as they got closer. *I think I recognize that guard..*

"NOW!" Anna yelled as she began to trap one of the guard's feet in a small gust of wind.

Emma moved the dirt under the guard's feet. They tried to defend themselves by sending bursts of air and dirt towards them. Emma subdued them easily, but not without giving several of them severe bruises and scrapes.

She looked down at the guard she'd recognized. She wondered if he knew all the things the locals were going through here in Alsager. He was from the Capital, and over there, things weren't this bad. The King didn't want chaos on his own doorstep, so perhaps this guard didn't understand why the rebels were fighting him. He was just another pawn in the King's game.

"Nice work!" Warren shouted as he hopped into the caravan and took the reins of the horses. "That was amazing! You should come with us on more missions."

Emma shrugged and climbed into the seat next to Warren. All they had to do was deliver the food to their contact in the city, and then it would go to the poor that desperately needed it. She felt good about helping the people, it was the first time in a long time she'd used her abilities against someone and not felt guilty.

Riding out along the edge of town, she watched as several people in rags cowered and hid as they drove by. They thought they were guards.

Emma sighed.

She imagined the lives these people had here. They had to constantly worry for their safety and if they'd have enough food to live through the week. She wanted to help them. She believed in what the rebels were doing, but she knew that stealing little bits of food wasn't enough. The King had to be stopped, but she didn't know if she could do it. She just wanted to get back to Zak and run away from everything, but how could she?

These people need me. Would Zak ever forgive me if I leave them to suffer?

The rest of the ride to the butcher, Emma tuned out the world around her. She didn't listen to Warren and Anna's conversation, but sat in silence while she contemplated what she should do.

CHAPTER 17

After a few weeks, the rebels seemed to accept Emma as one of them. She had proven her worth and was given the responsibility of leading missions to steal food for the nearby refugees.

"Are you nervous about your first mission with Qwen?" Anna asked as she brushed her long, silky hair out. "I've never done a mission with her. I'd be terrified."

Emma looked down at the worn piece of parchment in her hands. The edges of the paper were torn and folded, the words on it slightly faded. She'd been staring at it for the past few minutes while Anna had chatted, only half listening to what she was saying.

"I guess," she said, looking up briefly and shrugging. She sat on her bed waiting to leave for the mission, but her mind was elsewhere.

The letter was the last one she'd gotten from Zak. It had been three years since she had left him behind, and every day she wondered if she'd see him again. She rarely received updates on him anymore. She missed the first few months she was gone when she got letters from him every few weeks. This last letter was short, but it was the one that Emma had kept with her.

Emma,

I love you. This will be my last letter to you, I'm sorry. Thank you for everything you've done to try and protect me, but it's time I start doing things for myself. I'll never forget you. You are the best sister I could have ever hoped for. I miss you every day. Stay safe.

Love,
Zak

For months after receiving the letter, Emma had been furious. How could this be his last letter? It's not like he couldn't send them. The reports said he was still living in a small house on the seaside. He hadn't moved, he hadn't left; he just no longer wanted to write. Emma didn't understand why. The thought kept her awake at night as she wondered why he would make the decision of cutting off what little contact they still had between them. Didn't he know how much she missed him? It was heart wrenching.

Maybe something happened and they've been lying for years.

"Come on, it won't be that bad," Anna said as she sat on the bed next to Emma.

She smelled like lilacs and it reminded Emma of the fields outside Campton. Emma had taken Zak there during the summers whenever she didn't have to work. Those trips had been a rare break from their daily lives, and made them forget about their worries.

"I suppose so," Emma whispered as she refolded the parchment carefully. She tucked it into her breast pocket and looked back up at Anna. "I just want Qwen to like me, you know?"

Anna laughed.

"We all want that. It's hard, though. It always seems like an uphill battle with no results."

She looked at Emma and smiled.

"Let's go. Maybe you'll be the first of us she'll like."

They walked out of their room into the common area, where Qwen barked orders at some of the boys. Qwen seemed concerned that things would go wrong in her absence.

The air smelled richly of bacon fat and smoke. Emma's stomach grumbled, cursing her for missing breakfast. It would likely be quite a while before they would have a chance to eat, especially with Qwen leading the mission. From what Emma had heard, she was all business when she wanted something done. No time for food or rest until the job was done.

"There you are!" Qwen walked briskly towards them and stood next to Emma. "It's about time. We need to get going."

Emma nodded and shot Anna a worried look as she retreated to where Warren stood. He had been pretending to sweep while watching Qwen scold the others.

Qwen led Emma out of the common area towards two horses that were near the mouth of the cave. She thrust a satchel into Emma's hands before describing the tasks for the mission.

"There's food in there," she said. "You missed breakfast, and you'll need your strength. Eat up while you can."

Emma sighed with relief. She was glad she didn't have to ride on an empty stomach.

"We'll be taking these horses north of Alsager. Once we're there, we'll walk to a guardhouse just outside the city limits. Our intel says that Snelling will be on shift tonight. He's our target."

"Why are we targeting a guard?" Emma asked as she mounted her horse. He was a large chestnut quarter horse that kept moving around. Emma finally managed to keep him still before getting her foot in the stirrup and swinging up over the saddle.

Qwen sighed as if the answer was obvious.

"Snelling is one of the worst guards we've met. He's brutal. He has no problem beating and killing children for stealing bread. Everyone despises him, even some of the other guards. That's why we know he'll be there."

Emma wasn't thrilled about the idea of an assassination mission. It reminded her of the jobs she'd been sent on with the Royal Militia. She hated that people had to lose their lives over a pointless power struggle. It just wasn't right; If the King would just let the refugees live in peace, no one needed to die.

\#

The sun beat down on Charles' back, causing small beads of sweat to build up on his neck. He grabbed his handkerchief and dabbed at his forehead, cursing the sudden heat. It had been chilly when he'd left port today, so he'd worn a thick shirt and a leather jacket.

Now, as he stood waiting in the center of Alsager, he felt as if he were slowly roasting.

It had been three days since he'd last heard or seen any news of Emma. He'd been sitting outside a bakery having lunch when he saw a caravan drive by with her in the passenger seat. There had been several caravans ambushed by the rebels recently, so Charles had guessed that was his best chance at verifying whether Emma's cover story had worked. Based on how she was dressed and who she was with, he knew it had.

Now though, he was on a mission of his own. The King had kept him stationed close to where Emma was, but had some side projects brewing that needed a different kind of force. Charles was tasked with gaining the guards in Alsager's favor, to keep them on the side of the King.

Many years had passed since Charles had been sent on a mission for the King alone. He thought back to the month before the war had ended. He, the King and Queen Elizabeth had been on a boat headed back from Ban Lian. The political discussions had gone well, and the King was confident that they had reached a favorable agreement with the Emperor of Deoria. Charles was hopeful that this would be an end to the brutal war, now that the two leaders had finally come to fair terms.

His hope didn't last long, as shortly into their voyage back to Durisdeer, the King fell deathly ill. His body grew pale and weak, and his eyes began to glaze over with a milky haze.

It became obvious to everyone on the ship that he had been poisoned during the visit. The herb that had done it was a rare one from Deoria known as Ekronna. It often took days before the victim was affected by any symptoms, and by then their body would have started to decay, their systems shutting down. It was a gruesome death that could only be prevented with quick treatment by a skilled healer.

Queen Elizabeth was inconsolable as she watched helplessly while the King suffered. It would only take a few more days for the poison to kill him, and they were too far from Durisdeer to make it to a Royal Healer in time. Their only hope was to go back and find someone in Deoria.

Charles volunteered to take a boat back to Deoria and find a healer to help the King without drawing the Emperor's attention to their plight. They all knew that if King Marcell died, the war would continue and Deoria would eventually crush them.

At nightfall, Charles left the boat and headed back to shore. He was careful to hide his rowboat under several layers of leaves and branches so that it looked like washed up debris. Then, he made his way into the nearby city of Matadi.

The city was engulfed in flames when Charles arrived. He remembered the screams of the people, the smell of burning flesh in the air, and the taste of ash that coated his mouth and throat.

His eyes burned as he ran through the streets, trying to find any healer that was still alive. The only one he found was an old man that knelt outside a smoldering house. He sobbed into his hands and screamed unintelligibly.

"Sir," Charles ran to the man and tried to help him up. "Let me help you."

The man looked at Charles with teary hazel eyes and muttered, "There is no one left to help. Our Emperor has forsaken us."

"What do you mean? Who did this to you?" Charles screamed.

"The Emperor built a wall around Ban Lian, and left his people to burn. All of us that were blessed as Carbon elementalists have been sentenced to die."

The whole world seemed to grow still around Charles as he looked over the wreckage. The homes around him smoldered, and ash covered the night sky. He sat down next to the old man and listened to the stillness. He now knew what the agreement between the two men had been. They would destroy the cities of the Carbon elementalists, and cause thousands to die, but Ban Lian would remain safe. The Emperor would save his capital, but not the people.

#

A light breeze washed over them as they crouched behind a large row of hedges overlooking the hut where Snelling resided. It was a pleasant break from the heat of the autumn sun.

Emma watched their target: He was one of the guards that she'd seen the first time she'd gone into Alsager with Warren. He was the man that had stepped over the child like she was just a bug waiting to be squished. She had hated him then, and now, knowing the things that he had done, she hated him more. This was an assassination mission that she might not regret.

Her heart started to pound as they made their approach. Slowly, they pushed their way just in front of the hedges and began the sneak attack. Qwen led the assault by sending a swift burst of wind, littered with small, jagged pieces of iron towards the unsuspecting guard.

Just as Qwen's attack was about to hit, Snelling cocked his head and frowned.

He flicked his wrist and deflected the blow using his own abilities. Emma didn't quite understand what had happened as she followed up Qwen's blow with one of her own, but something was wrong. Their intel had said the guard was strong, but not an elementalist.

Emma watched as he defended their blows effortlessly and she began to worry. They weren't prepared for a real fight.

Qwen groaned. They hadn't expected it to be easy, but they had no idea that Snelling was one of them. They would have to improvise now.

Emma saw the guard move to strike back. He made a small whirlwind out of the iron shrapnel and prepared to launch it at them. Adrenaline pulsed through her veins as she shoved Qwen out of the way.

A small piece of metal sliced her wrist. It cut deep into her skin and sent a steady flow of blood onto the ground around her. Emma winced and grabbed her wrist to slow the bleeding.

The seconds seemed like minutes as her wrist burned. The pain seared and spread up and down her arm. The rapid blood loss made her feel dizzy, and she tried to focus her attention on the guard, who was preparing another attack.

"I don't understand," Qwen said, her voice gruff. "How could our source be wrong about this? He's a damn elementalist."

She sighed and whipped the air around them at the guard, trying to knock him off balance. He fought back skillfully, his counter attacks danced playfully with Qwen's. He was having no trouble fending off Qwen's moves, and it was clear from the execution of his tactics that he had years of experience fighting.

He smirked at them as he knocked Qwen back again with a forceful wall of wind. Her body smacked loudly against the earth as her legs gave out on her.

Emma cringed at the sound of her head hitting the rock. Surely she'd be knocked out from that blow, if not worse.

They were losing.

Qwen is unconcious, I can just kill him.

Emma exhaled and took two steps forward as she stared the guard down. Their eyes met, a shared flicker of determination between them. She allowed her body to feel the air around her, the elements that circled between them, the blood pulsing through the guard's veins. Everything started to feel familiar, each piece began to take shape in her mind. Time slowed down as she pictured the attack in her head.

It was something that Dominic had taught her: focus on the elements, and then rip their bonds apart. She thought about the blood in the guard, a mixture of chemical compounds that she could manipulate: plasma, water, blood cells, oxygen, carbon dioxide.

Dominic had explained that not everything was a simple chemical equation, that some were a complex combination.

Under his training, Emma had learned how to concentrate on the pieces and then recalibrate her attention to the whole. She knew she could manipulate his blood, even if she wasn't a chemist. She could sense the elements calling to her.

With a hold on the chemicals in his body, Emma felt that he was about to attack again. She could feel his muscles tense. The blood pulsed through his heart and raced through his body as he moved.

Now.

With a single thought, she broke apart the organs that kept his blood pumping. In an instant, he fell to the ground. His eyes rolled to the back of his head as blood spilled from his nose and mouth.

#

Qwen's head was spinning. It felt like a boulder had crushed the air out of her lungs. Agony pulsed through her neck and back as she laid on the ground.

"Are you okay?" Emma said. She knelt beside her. "Qwen, can you hear me?"

Qwen tried to nod, but even a slight movement of her head caused her to feel sick. She could feel the hot bile burning her throat as she tried to keep herself from vomiting. After several deep breaths, she spoke.

"Yeah, I'll be fine."

It had been a long time since she'd been beaten in a fight, and nothing about this made sense. How could she have been struck down, yet Emma was almost completely uninjured? Maybe she had been wrong about this scrawny little thing. Maybe she was a decent fighter after all. At the very least, she had the attitude for it; she was stubborn.

Slowly, Qwen pushed herself up. Everything around them seemed quiet, and the night sky grew dark. Her eyes fell on the guard's fallen body a few yards away from her. Blood dripped from his mouth and nostrils. His eyes were a brilliant shade of red. She'd only ever seen one person look like that after they'd died, and that was years ago when she was a new rebel recruit.

"How did you do that?" She asked.

"I don't know," Emma whispered timidly. "I just reacted and shot a burst of air at him. I think I may have given him a heart attack or something."

Her voice cracked as she spoke. Qwen wondered if this was the first person the girl had ever killed, but something about the way she looked made her doubt it. It was quick and precise, but definitely not a heart attack.

"I'm just glad you beat him," Qwen sighed. She looked at Emma, who smiled sheepishly back. "We'll rest a few minutes and then head back, okay?"

While they sat in the grass, Emma pulled out two small canteens of water from her bag. She handed one to Qwen and began to drink from the other. They sat in silence and drank while Qwen regained her balance.

Qwen thought to herself as she looked at the guard.

This isn't a coincidence. She must be hiding something.

"Could you do me a favor and bring me my pack? I think it fell over there." Qwen said as her hand reached to her back pocket. Her fingers wrapped carefully around a small vial that she had tucked away. She carefully pulled it out while Emma stood up to get the pack.

As stealthily as she could manage, Qwen grabbed Emma's canteen and unscrewed the cap. Emma reached the pack just as Qwen poured a few drops from the vial into the water, and quickly re-sealed it. She placed it back down on the ground as Emma turned around, the small burlap sack in her hands.

"Thanks," Qwen said as she placed the vial back in her pocket. "I should be okay to go soon. Let's rest a bit more, then head back."

Emma nodded and took another drink from her canteen.

#

The air was crisp and smelled like rain, the only sound was the clomping of hooves as they rode. Emma breathed in the scent of the forest. She'd always loved running in the woods with Zak as a child. It made her feel peaceful, like nothing bad could happen while they stood amongst the tall embrace of the trees.

It had been almost an hour since they had buried the guard and left to return to base. Emma had worried that Qwen would be skeptical about how she had defeated the guard, but it seemed that she was just happy to be finished with the mission. So far, she hadn't questioned her or said anything that showed her she was suspicious. Emma thought about how her head had smashed on the ground, and she wondered if it had caused more damage than she was letting on.

"Are you feeling okay?" Emma asked.

As she asked it, she realized that she was feeling a bit weak herself. She placed a hand on the horse's shoulder to balance herself.

"Yeah," Qwen said. "Just tired. How are you doing?"

Emma's head started to spin. She was fine a moment ago, but now she was having a hard time keeping herself upright in the saddle. Everything was hazy, but she could see that Qwen was smirking slightly.

What's happening? I'm losing my balance.

"I'm suddenly really dizzy..."

"It's about time," Qwen said.

She pulled the reins of her horse and came to a halt as Emma slid limply off the saddle. Her head thumped as she hit the ground.

"That took longer than it should have. You really are a tough one after all."

Emma's heart pounded in her temples. Her body burned as she lay motionless. She couldn't speak; her mouth wouldn't move. She could only watch as Qwen got off her horse and stood over her.

"I'm sorry to do this," she said as she picked up Emma's body and laid it sideways across the horse's back. Qwen was much stronger than she thought. "But I know you didn't kill that guard with air. You are a carbon elementalist. I can't take you back to base."

She felt like a prisoner in her own body. Nothing responded. She felt her heart thumping, her blood pumping through her veins, but nothing worked. Her entire body had shut down, incapable of movement.

She's going to kill me. Why were you so reckless? If only I could move.

Emma's mind raced as she realized that this could be the end. She was completely vulnerable, and they were no longer headed in the direction of the base. She had no idea where Qwen was taking her as they continued through the dark woods.

Then, Emma felt it, like a wave of acid pumping through her veins. If she focused all her energy on her blood, she could sense the poison as it moved through her. She could feel the chemical compositions and all the bonds that held them together. If she concentrated hard enough, she might be able to pull at them to break the chemicals down.

Emma focused desperately on the poison.

Her head spun as she used what little energy she had left on breaking apart the chemical bonds.

Emma's body began to tingle. She could feel sensations in her fingertips again and move them ever so slightly.

It was working; she was slowly breaking down the poison inside her.

I hope this works before it's too late.

They rode for almost an hour and Emma was exhausted from the intense concentration. Her mind drifted off and her attention waned as her body bounced along with the steps of the horse.

The horse slowed down, but Emma didn't notice until they had come to a complete stop. There was a light in the corner of her eye that flickered against the darkness. A fire burned in the woods; they had come across someone out here.

Is this where Qwen is taking me?

"Who's there?" A young man's voice called to them from near the fire.

Emma couldn't see what he looked like. She thought she could turn her head now, but she didn't dare show Qwen that she was able to move. Not yet.

Qwen jumped off her horse and called back, "It's Qwen. I need to talk to you."

"Who's with you?"

Emma could hear the rustling of leaves as he walked towards them.

"A new recruit," Qwen stated plainly. "I think she's a carbon elementalist. We were on a mission and she killed a guard. It was like she turned his insides to liquid, causing him to bleed and fall without any injuries to the outside. I've never seen anyone do that except…"

A pause lingered between them. Her voice shook and she seemed to choke on her words.

"Me."

"Yes," Qwen said. "What should we do with her, Captain?"

Emma's heart pounded in her throat. She had never met another carbon elementalist, and she had always wondered if they'd all been killed off except for her.

The Captain is a carbon elementalist? Does the King know? Is that why he really sent me? Am I the only person that can beat him?

Now might be her only chance if she was going to kill him. He and Qwen thought she was paralyzed; she could seize the moment and take them by surprise, kill them both and make a run for it.

The King would finally have what he wanted, and maybe he wouldn't come searching for her. She would be able to leave Durisdeer for good, find Zak and put everything behind her to start a new life.

"Kill her," he said. "We can't risk it."

Qwen shifted her weight and turned towards Emma.

"Okay," Qwen whispered. "I'm sorry."

Instinctively, Emma twisted her body out of the way just as Qwen moved to stab her.

The blade hit the saddle, causing the horse to rear back and bolt away from them. Emma used the distraction to quickly jump to her feet and face her opponents.

"Interesting," the young man said calmly. If he was surprised, he didn't show it. Emma couldn't see his face in the shadows, but she could tell he was smirking. "You're clever to break down the paralysis poison so quickly. It's a shame we can't use you in the rebellion. It's just too risky. No hard feelings, I hope."

Emma was still weak from the poison. Her body shook as she stood.

She tried to feel the other carbon elementalist's pulse so she could grasp the elements that made him. It felt fuzzy. She couldn't quite grab a hold of them.

They slipped through her focus every time she tried to concentrate, like the elements were just out of reach.

"You've never dueled a carbon elementalist, have you?" He scoffed. "I can feel what you're trying to do. I can block you. Can you do that?"

Emma felt the muscles in her body tighten. She fell to her knees and clutched at her chest. It felt like her heart was being crushed by a fist. Her breaths became louder as she inhaled and exhaled deeply to compensate for the oxygen that left her body.

She could feel the elements inside of her moving, and she tried to move them back to normal by focusing on her pulse. Her body felt like it was on fire as heat spread through her veins.

Is this what I do to people?

It took all of her strength to keep him from killing her. Her body felt like it was about to give out any second, but she refused to let up. She needed to be strong.

"You're an impressive fighter," he said. He took a few steps closer towards her. "I really am sorry about this, but we have to make sacrifices to stop the King."

He continued to pull apart at her body, ripping every piece of tissue and muscle he could. She felt her organs ache and tremble while blood dripped from her nose. She wondered how much longer she could keep him from killing her.

Her heartbeat slowed.

She saw flashes of white each time she blinked. Her body grew weaker and weaker as her opponent overpowered her. He continued to step closer towards her until the light from the fire finally illuminated his face.

She recognized him as soon as he stepped into view.

He was older, but the outline of his tousled black hair shone against the burning flames. His deep, hazel eyes and spindly lashes were unmistakable.

Emma felt time stand still. She could no longer hear the crackling of the fire, only the beating of her own heart.

She stopped fighting back.

"Zak?"

CHAPTER 18

Just like that, their routine had been broken. Every day, Emma would get up just after the sun rose and go into the city to find food. When she returned, she would wake Zak up, and together they would eat whatever Emma had been lucky enough to find. After breakfast she'd leave for a long day of work on the fishing boat.

Each day seemed to flow into the next, and each day was predictable. That day, though, was different. She'd come back from the city with two loaves of bread and a chunk of slightly moldy cheese, only to find that Zak was missing.

"Zak?" She called out frantically, cupping her hands to the sides of her mouth.

Their neighbours watched as Emma began to panic. She ran back and forth along the rafts towards land, screaming his name.

It took almost an hour before Emma found Zak sitting by the shore, gazing into the distance as he watched the floating homes bob with the waves. He rested comfortably, sitting on the ground with his back against the trunk of a tree. His legs were outstretched lazily.

In his hand was a piece of chicken. His fingers and lips were coated with a shiny layer of grease. As Emma approached, a wide toothy smile spread across his face.

"Want some?" He asked as he handed her a piece. "I saved you the legs."

Emma was speechless, a look of confusion on her face. How on earth had he managed to get this?

"I could smell it from our raft," Zak said. He lifted his right arm up and wiped chicken fat from his chin with his sleeve. "So I waited until the man a few rafts down was distracted, then I snatched it and ran."

He took another large bite of meat and chewed happily.

"You... you stole this?" She asked slowly. Her little brother was not as innocent as she thought.

Zak nodded.

"From another refugee's raft?"

He nodded again and took another bite.

Emma sighed and sat down beside him, pushing away the chicken leg he offered to her.

"We can't steal from the poor, Zak," she said quietly. "They're no better off than us. We're all the same – we're all just fighting to survive. Can you promise me not to do that again?"

Zak looked up at his older sister.

"But we need food to live. What else can we eat? We have almost nothing."

"Just promise me. We're better than that," Emma gulped, hoping she sounded confident enough to hide the fact that stealing food in the city was what she did at times when money was tight.

Zak looked pensive for a moment, and then nodded as he reached to tear off another piece of chicken. Emma couldn't tell if he understood.

Sometimes, Emma wondered if keeping him away from the unfairness of the world was the right thing to do. So far, she had always shielded him from the city's troubles. Other 8-year-old boys begged in the streets and stole from merchants, but he sat by the sea, reading stories and playing made-up games or skipping rocks.

At the end of each day, he spent time with Emma talking about why the sky was blue or how the clouds were made. At least, this was all she thought he did. Now, she wasn't so sure. What did he really do while she was away?

Their reunion wasn't what Emma imagined it would be. After recognizing Zak during their fight, she'd passed out. The next thing she knew, she woke up in a bed with Zak sitting beside her.

He stared out the window, his chin resting on his palm. His breathing was loud and heavy and there was a distant look of anguish in his eyes. He let out a small sigh.

"It's really you," Emma whispered, her voice croaked. She reached her hand out to brush her fingertips along the hem of his sleeve.

This must be a dream.

"Yeah," he said, turning his gaze away from the window and looking at her. "And it's really you."

Over the past few years, Emma had imagined seeing him again so many times. Every so often, she invented scenarios in her mind of reuniting with Zak and all the things they would tell each other after having spent so long apart. Now she had no idea what to say. It wasn't at all what she had expected.

He was just Zak; young, sweet, naive Zak. He was supposed to be her baby brother forever, not the powerful, feared captain of the rebels.

"I know this is hard for you to accept, and I know this is a shock," he said. "I hope you can forgive me for not taking the path you wanted. I just had to do something. I had to help."

Emma nodded. She wasn't angry to see her brother here, but she certainly wasn't happy either. She felt numb and confused.

"When I came back to our raft that morning after you left, I found your note, and I was furious that you abandoned me. For days, I cried and hid. I cursed you for leaving me behind like that. I thought I would never forgive you."

Emma's heart ached as she imagined Zak sobbing alone in the dead of night, no one around to comfort him. She thought about how selfish she had been to desert him and how heartbroken he must have been.

"But I went into the city and for the first few months I lived in a small house. I had a simple life, and a much easier one compared to our days on the raft," Zak tried to maintain his composure, but he quivered as he spoke.

"Living in the city, I was surrounded by people suffering. From my own window, I could see mothers pacing up and down the streets from dawn to dusk, asking everyone who walked by for food. Little kids not far from my age just sat around, hungry and helpless."

He paused and stared down at the ground for a few seconds before continuing.

"I couldn't stand it...just seeing all of it made me so angry. Why was life so unfair? These people hadn't done anything wrong. They didn't deserve to be poor. One day, I snapped. A guard was whipping a little boy for stealing bread, and without really thinking, I stopped him. I didn't know how at the time, but looking back now... it was so easy to control him. Soon, it dawned on me that I had the ability to manipulate people like this. I had the power to control the elements inside them. It was then – it was then that I realized I could do something more."

Emma reached over and placed her hand on his.

"Is that when you started this group of rebels?"

"Not right away," he said. "I worked on my own for a bit, slinking around in the shadows, trying not to draw attention to myself. I thought that would be enough. And then I met Qwen. We understood each other and she was so much like me, but wiser and older. She reminded me of you."

Zak looked at Emma. His eyes looked weary and full of sadness.

"At that time, she was putting together a small group of rebels, and I joined them. She was the real leader all along. But I was the one with the gold and power to get things really going."

It all started to make sense – the gold that she'd left him had been used to get the rebellion really started. Her brother had teamed up with Qwen and started training a militia to take on the guards and end their corruption.

"So that's how it all started? You financed the rebellion, and the two of you trained the new recruits?" Emma asked.

"Yes," he said. "It didn't take long before we were recruiting a few dozen people a week. Everyone was tired of the corruption, which made it easy for us to grow. Most people wanted in. Now, we have a few thousand people throughout the country. Each group acts mostly on its own and they all have their individual leaders, but every now and then, Qwen or I send out larger orders."

"So you aren't heavily involved day to day anymore?"

"Not really, which is probably news to the King and his militia," Zak replied. He swallowed twice, then rubbed his eyes with the backs of his hands. "He's wanted to take me out since he realized what was happening, but really, I'm just a small cog in the machine now. If they get me, which, is just a matter of time, it wouldn't make much of a difference to the rebels' operations. Everything would still go on as is."

"No," Emma said loudly. "You can't let him kill you! I finally have you back, Zak. We should run away and start a new life, leave all of this behind for good. Qwen can lead the rebels. We don't have to be part of this mess anymore."

Zak looked away and walked slowly to the window. He interlaced his fingers and rested both elbows on the thick stone ledge as he stared outside.

"He'd burn cities to the ground trying to find me, Emma. You know that," he said quietly, not turning around to face her. "He'd track us until he had my body, lifeless, in his hands. He'd send more people like you to find us, and more innocents would end up dead in the process. I already have a lot on my conscience. I can't live with more."

"How did you know he sent me?" She asked.

Zak turned around, leaning against the window.

"I knew they were training you. They described a girl who had similar powers to me, and our ability to manipulate elements is so rare. I've only met one other carbon elementalist, and he's at the bottom of the sea. I was sure it had to be you the King was training. I just didn't think he'd send you so soon. I can't believe I almost killed you…"

Emma wanted to stop him and ask about the other carbon elementalist, but he continued.

"The guards wanted to cut off all connection between us, so I knew they wouldn't tell you what I was up to after I stopped checking in with them. But they wanted you to continue fighting for them – you're the strongest they've ever had – so they lied to keep you happy. I'm sure they told you I was safely tucked away somewhere after I stopped writing. After our fight yesterday, I realized it made perfect sense they'd send you. You wouldn't know it was me, and since the King knows I'm a carbon elementalist, you had the best chance of defeating me. He probably thought you wouldn't recognize me after all these years."

"Then he's an idiot, of course I'd recognize you," Emma said slowly. She couldn't help smiling as she thought of how much Zak had grown, of what a wise, young man he had become. "I'm so proud of you Zak. But you know we can't stay here."

"I know," he said. "Not while the King is alive."

Emma nodded.

"Join me, Emma. Help me take the King down from our side. You'll be able to get closer to him than I ever could, and if we take him out, the Kingdom will finally be able to heal."

He looked at Emma with a determination that she had never seen before in his eyes.

Emma stayed quiet for a while. It had been a long day, and she was overwhelmed with the shock of seeing Zak and hearing all that he had done. She needed to think it through.

"We would be a team of carbon elementalists working together. The only thing that can stop us is each other," Zak continued, interrupting the silence between them. "Together we're as powerful as any army."

Emma thought to herself about the life she had in the Capital. Jason, Adam, Charles, all of the people she'd have to leave behind if she agreed. She had grown attached to them through the years... But it was Zak. She had missed him so much, and he was right. She had to kill the King.

#

The following morning Emma woke up to the smell of bacon cooking on the fire crackling outside of Zak's cabin. He'd checked on her multiple times in the night, and it made her think of all the times she had taken care of him years ago.

"Zak?" Emma called as she sat up.

He poked his head in the door and looked at her.

"I'm glad you're finally awake." He said. His voice was so much deeper than she remembered it. "Do you feel up to eating?"

Emma's stomach lurched at the thought of food. She hadn't eaten anything since the rations Qwen had shoved at her. She nodded and forced herself out of bed.

Light blinded her as she stepped outside, it was already afternoon and there were no clouds blocking the sun. She placed a hand above her eyes as she stepped out towards a pair of small chairs.

"Come eat," Zak said. He motioned to one of the chairs and the skillet that rested near the fire.

The crispy bacon made her mouth water as she bit into it. The salt and fat coated her fingertips as she ate piece after piece. Zak watched her as she ate, and smiled.

"I'm glad I got to see you again, Emma. I was worried that one of us would be killed before we'd cross paths."

Emma set down her food and smiled at him.

"Me too. I never stopped thinking about you. Or worrying."

Zak laughed.

"You always worried too much."

"I had to protect you!"

"No Zak, don't touch the water. No Zak, don't run that fast. Don't go into the city. Don't read at night, it'll hurt your eyes." He smiled widely as he mocked her.

"I've missed this," Emma said.

She couldn't remember the last time she'd been this content. Even though she knew she'd have to go back to Portishead and face the King, in this moment life was perfect.

"Were you always this brave?" She asked.

His eyebrows furrowed a little. His face was much more masculine than she remembered it, he'd grown a lot in the past few years. He didn't look 15 to her, and he definitely wasn't the little boy she had so many memories of.

"No." Zak stared at his feet. "When you first left I was terrified. It took a long time before I was willing to go outside my new house for more than a few minutes. I knew they'd taken you, and I thought they'd come for me too."

"Why? Why would they have come for you?"

"Because I'm a carbon elementalist too. Didn't you know back then?"

He looked at her, confused.

Did he know when we were kids?

"I didn't know what it really meant until I first killed that guard," he said. "But even when you were still with me, I knew I was an elementalist. I used to play with the water and the air on the raft. Shortly before you left I started moving branches and logs, just because I could."

Emma couldn't believe it. She never realized he had powers when they were younger. How had she not noticed?

"I'm amazed at how strong you are," she said. "I've been beaten before, but never like that."

Zak shrugged.

"When Qwen and I started out, we came across an old man that was also a carbon elementalist. His name was Aaron. He was my friend and mentor for several months."

Zak paused and frowned.

"What happened?"

"Once the rebellion started to pick up, he grew power hungry. He wanted to start using our group and our powers for his own gains. He didn't really care about helping people, he just wanted to make his own life better. It was a little over a year ago when he tried to kill me by surprise using what I did to you earlier. Qwen snuck up on him and distracted him. We managed to barely beat him by working together, but it came at a cost."

He lifted his shirt and showed off several long, deep purple scars that ran the length of his torso.

"Qwen has several as well, and ever since we've been very wary of anyone joining our ranks."

Emma nodded.

It made sense now why Qwen was so standoffish to newcomers. She expected that day was still burned into her memory.

"Have you ever met anyone else like us?" Emma asked.

She had always thought she was the only one. But now Zak, and this other man. Maybe there were more.

"No."

Emma's heart sank a little. She had hoped maybe there was a place she and Zak would be welcomed to once this was all over, but it didn't matter as long as they were together.

The wind played with the dirt on the ground as they sat and finished eating. Emma wished she could pause this moment sitting with Zak, and hold onto it forever. She didn't want to go back to reality.

\#

Emma stood up straight and held her head high with her shoulders back. Adrenaline rushed through her veins. She had rehearsed her speech for hours, and it was finally time.

The King sat in front of her, lounging comfortably in his throne. He barely glanced at Emma, as if she were a speck of dust floating around the room.

"You can't continue to hunt the rebels. There's no use," she said. Her voice echoed confidently through the room as it bounced off the stone walls of the chamber. "They're only trying to protect the poor from starvation, and from your corrupted guards."

The King scowled.

"How dare you?" He said loudly. "You come back from an unsuccessful mission, and tell me, the King, what I must do?"

"You knew the captain of the rebels was Zak when you sent me," she replied. "You asked me to kill my own brother for your foolish pride."

"I didn't ask you. I ordered, and you failed."

"No. You are the one who failed. As a King, you've failed your people. For years, my brother has been trying to clean up the mess, the mess that you won't admit to."

"Those filthy beggars aren't my people," he yelled. He leaned forward in his seat. "They should never have fled here. Why should my citizens be responsible for feeding and clothing another countries' rejects?"

Every muscle tensed in Emma and she felt the blood rush to her head.

How can anyone be so cruel, so heartless?

It took everything in her to keep from lashing out and crushing his throat. He didn't deserve to live, let alone have the power to govern a kingdom.

"So you'd rather innocent people died than provide them with food and water? You'd let their children go hungry and die in the streets so that you can save money?"

"Yes."

He folded his hands in his lap and nodded.

"If the refugees died off, my people would be better off for it. My duty is to them, not to the poor and helpless that just happened to wash up on our shores."

"How can you be so cruel?" She cried out, no longer able to keep her emotions under control. It was infuriating that anyone could be so selfish and stubborn when so many lives were at stake. "How can you let the children die? They're innocent. They've done nothing to you!"

"Do not speak to me as if you are my equal, you little bitch!"

He jumped to his feet and thrust a pointed finger in her direction. His voice thundered in the chamber.

"You may be powerful, but I can still have you executed for treason! I've had enough of this nonsense."

Emma laughed.

"I'd like to see you or any of your guards try to kill me."

"Guards! Take her to the prison."

A row of guards marched into the room from behind the throne. They wore royal purple uniforms and had loud, metal boots that clacked as they hit the floor.

The guards shared the same serious expression on their faces. Their brows furrowed and their eyes stared straight ahead. Emma recognized them as the King's elite squad, and was surprised to see them in a group. Typically they would each be split up and sent on different solo missions. The King had planned this; he wanted her to rot in his prison until she gave in to his demands and served him blindly. He was throwing everything he had at her.

As the guards advanced towards her, Emma dropped down into a lowered fighting stance. She focused on the elements in the room around her as she looked at the guards and the King.

This is it. He has to die.

A single line of candles flickered against the side of the room. Emma closed her eyes and pulled the air around the room into giant concentric circles. The air whipped through the flames and blended the fire into the small whirlwind.

In one swift motion, she flung the circles of fire towards the guards and the King, causing a wall of smoke that spun and hissed wildly to come between them.

The room heated as tapestries and furniture caught on fire. The air in the room grew thick, making it hard to breathe.

Emma didn't care about maintaining control. She let herself give in to the fire's chaos as flames licked furiously at the walls. The flames grew larger as they spread around the room. Several guards fought the flames by manipulating the oxygen around themselves and the King. They made shields of wind to keep the fire at bay. As the fire grew they struggled to maintain their defense.

Emma blocked everything out of her mind to focus on targeting her attacks directly at the King. She sent whips of fire and wind flying in his direction, hoping to engulf him in flames. The guards continued to deflect them and launch counter attacks towards her.

Without concern for her own safety, Emma did little to divert the blows. A piece of metal cut her stomach, and she felt herself being burned on her arms and neck. Emma winced, but didn't let the pain distract her. Blood seeped out from the cut as the fire sucked desperately at the oxygen in the room. Everything was covered in smoke and ash.

Her body tensed and in a moment of intense concentration, she shot out a wave of energy that made the guards collapse to the ground. As they lay motionless, blood dripped from their noses and mouths. They weren't dead, but they were severely injured and had internal bleeding. Emma had hoped to avoid this violence, but it wasn't possible anymore. She couldn't let the King escape justice.

Now, with the guards disabled, Emma forced herself forward towards the King. He stood and stared down at her with his beady eyes. His body heaved up and down as he took deep breaths.

"You'll regret this one day," he warned.

"I'm willing to risk it."

A trickle of blood ran down her fingers to the ground as she raised her hand at him. With her arm outstretched, she curled her fingers into a choking motion. Using all the energy she could summon, she focused on her arm and pulled it backwards to draw the air out of the King's lungs.

His body fought her as she controlled his lungs to suffocate him. He flailed and grabbed at his chest. He couldn't stop her.

Suddenly, a shadow emerged from the corner of her eye.

Footsteps clattered against the floor.

Jason.

He lunged at the King and knocked him to the ground, breaking Emma's concentration and allowing him to regain his breath. Jason stood up and looked at Emma.

"I don't want to fight you, Emma," he said calmly. "I hate my father, but this isn't the right way to fix things."

Rage pulsed through her. She was so close; she could feel the life leaving him. She imagined him taking his last breath as he crumbled to the floor, just like all the innocent lives lost during the missions he had sent her on.

Why is he interfering?

"I have to," Emma cried.

"No. You don't," Jason said.

He paused. His eyes darted to the floor and back up again.

"Not yet. Leave and save your brother. My father sent a team to kill him when he heard you were returning. You have to go now."

Everything came to a standstill as Emma took in what Jason had just said.

She felt numb. Zak was in danger. She'd lost him once, and she wasn't going to lose him again. Killing the King was important, but nothing was more important to her than her brother.

She had to hurry.

CHAPTER 19

Screams echoed through the hallway as Adam and Charles approached the throne room. They had rushed over as soon as they'd heard Emma was in the Capital. Something must have happened, she had to be here. The thick oak doors of the throne room were locked from the inside. Charles looked warily at Adam and pressed his ear against the door.

Minutes passed before the door finally swung open with such force that it slammed against the wall. A bloody and bruised Emma limped out past them, her eyes bloodshot and her face burned. As she exited the room, she looked around cautiously as if she were expecting someone to attack her.

"What did you do?" Charles said.

"I had to kill the King," Emma replied slowly.

She barely opened her mouth as she spoke. Unable to support her weight any longer, she sat down on the floor and looked up to meet Charles' eyes.

"But Jason stopped me. They're sending a team to kill Zak. He's the captain. I have to get there before they do."

"I'm going with you," Adam said as he placed an arm gently around her waist.

"No, it's too dangerous."

Emma chewed on her bottom lip.

"Exactly. That's why you need me. Look at yourself, you're already half dead. You can barely move. I won't let you go alone."

"Whoever is going, you need to go now," Charles said flatly, interrupting their conversation. He paced as he spoke. "It won't be long before they send anyone the King can find after you now, and they'll put me in charge. The King doesn't know I'm helping you, so I'll do what I can to slow them down. I'll lead them there by sea. The currents at this time of day will buy us a little time."

Emma opened her mouth to protest, but Charles cut her off and pointed down the hall.

"We'll talk later," he said firmly. "Adam, go get a horse from the stables and do what you need to do to get her out of here. Now."

In one quick motion, Adam lifted Emma up and balanced her on his shoulder. Her body was almost fully limp, and she was still losing a good amount of blood. Her eyes rolled to the side and she struggled to stay awake. He had to hurry to get her out of the city so that he could properly treat her.

Why is she always so reckless?

Adam wondered if she even cared about surviving. He couldn't imagine how heartbreaking this was for her, learning that her brother was the leader of the rebels and that she had spent the past several years of her life being trained to kill him. He wished he could take her far away from all of this, somewhere safe where she could start over and just live a peaceful life. After all she had gone through, she deserved that. She deserved to be happy for once.

It only took a few minutes of running before they reached the stables. Adam's heartbeat raced as he lowered Emma slowly to the ground, careful not to hurt her. Looking around, he grabbed the nearest saddle and placed it on the back of a strong chestnut mare.

Once the saddle was securely attached, he grabbed a few bags of feed and hooked them to the horse before propping Emma's semi-conscious body onto it's back.

It would be tricky, but his plan was to ride the horse with her gingerly balanced over the front of the saddle until she was strong enough to steady herself again. Emma didn't look like she would regain consciousness any time soon, but there was no other choice.

Adam headed quickly out of the capital, trying not to attract attention. It was almost impossible, though, with an unconscious girl on his horse. A few people looked at him, their eyebrows raised as they whispered to one another. Luckily for him the average citizen cared more about staying out of trouble than helping a stranger. It was a depressing fact that he'd come to accept about the city, but today he was grateful for it.

Alsager was normally just a few hours' ride away, but unless Emma woke up soon, he expected it would take most of the day. With Emma precariously balanced on the horse, he could only ride at a slow, steady pace. She might fall off if the horse began to gallop, and that wasn't a risk he was willing to take.

The road twisted out of the city and the clean cobblestones became patches of mud and dirt. Farm fields stretched far into the distance and the sun beat down brightly, casting a glimmer over the grass. Adam couldn't help but notice how the sun rays illuminated Emma's face, her skin glowed in the light.

Once they were out of the city, Adam pulled the horse to a halt. More than half an hour had already passed. Emma's wounds needed to be dealt with now that they wouldn't be spotted.

Emma began to stir slightly as Adam stopped the horse, her eyes fluttered open. Adam gently pushed a stray strand of hair behind her ear. She looked up at him, dazed and confused.

"Emma," he whispered. "Just relax. It's okay. You're safe."

Emma looked around and blinked a few times. She tried to lower herself off the horse, wincing in pain as Adam slid off the saddle to help her.

"Where are we?" She asked. Her voice cracked as she spoke.

"Hold still," Adam said as he stood alongside the horse to help her get down. "We're on the road to Alsager, but we need to take care of your wounds before going any further."

Adam extended a hand to Emma as she dismounted slowly.

She laid flat on the dirt as soon as she was off the horse. Her face scrunched with pain.

"You have a few cuts I need to look at. They're deep, so we have to be careful," Adam said as he grabbed his medical bag off the side of the saddle. "Where does it hurt?"

Emma laughed softly, her chuckle barely audible.

"Everywhere."

Adam knelt down beside her and grabbed a stack of cotton squares and a small vial filled with a healing salve. He had been training as a medic for years, but this was the first time treating anyone so severely injured. He wasn't sure if he was prepared for this, but he was her best hope. Spots of blood soaked through her thin linen shirt and pants. He swallowed nervously.

"I'm going to have to clean these wounds and bandage them," Adam said as he pulled up the bottom of her shirt. He held his breath, expecting the worse.

He lifted the fabric to expose a large gash that covered the lower half of her belly. It was deep, and still bleeding. The area around it was brown and crusted with dried blood.

Emma nodded and looked away as he started to clean the wound. Her body tensed while Adam pressed against her abdomen, working the salve slowly into the wound while applying steady pressure to stop the bleeding. He knew how much she was hurting and took special care not to press down too hard.

It didn't take long for the salve to begin working. In a matter of minutes, the bleeding had stopped. It was almost a miracle what the medicines that Dominic had developed could do. They could stop bleeding from most wounds in a few minutes, and cause cell regeneration to double in speed. With the salve, injuries would fully heal in a third of the time, sometimes faster.

"There. Is that a bit better?" Adam asked as he pulled Emma's shirt back down to cover her stomach.

He couldn't help but notice how toned her muscles were. He fought back thoughts of getting closer to her or brushing her hair back affectionately. This wasn't the right time or place. He wasn't sure what would be, but this definitely wasn't. Adam snapped out of his thoughts and looked at Emma.

"Let's see if you can stand up."

Shakily, Emma got to her feet. She balanced herself against Adam, gripping his shoulder as firmly as she could. She was weak from the blood loss, but she was regaining some of her strength now.

"I think I'm okay to ride," she said as she twisted her torso slightly to test her range of motion. "It hurts, but I'll manage."

Adam helped her mount the horse. Her body was still shaking, but she managed to hold herself upright while he got on behind her. He reached around her and grabbed the reins, pulling them away from the horse's long auburn hair. He gripped them firmly as they began to move again. Emma navigated them the rest of the way to her brother's hideout.

#

"Zak!" Emma exclaimed.

He was slumped against a wooden chair. An empty crystal vial laid on the ground just in front of him. Emma ran to him.

"What have you done?"

She grabbed Zak's face firmly between her hands and looked at him. His eyes were half closed, and his skin was pale and cold to the touch. He barely moved, his entire body weight sunk deep into the chair.

"Zak!" She repeated, her voice dripped with desperation. He looked like he was on the verge of death.

"I - I had to," he said shakily.

His speech was slow and Emma could tell he was struggling to get the words out.

"They'd never stop. I'd always be something they could use against you."

Emma shook her head frantically as tears filled her eyes. She couldn't believe her brother was taking his own life.

"No, we could have done something together," she cried.

Zak smiled weakly. The corners of his mouth were slightly upturned but sadness rested in his eyes.

"I raised a rebellion," he said quietly, as if this was a secret between the two of them. He took a deep breath. "Now you and Qwen are free to finish what I started - the rebels will be outraged when Qwen tells them I'm dead - they'll launch an assault within a month on the Capital. The King won't be prepared."

Zak put his palm on his chest and grimaced in pain. "But -"

"It's already planned Emma."

A slight breeze blew over them and he shivered. His teeth clattered weakly.

"There's no turning back now - I'm dying."

Emma sat down on the floor next to him and grabbed his icy hand. His breathing was shallow and strained, and his eyes couldn't focus as he looked at her.

"After I die, please take my body to the King," Zak stammered. "Tell him you killed me. We'll need someone on the inside when the rebels attack."

"He'll know I didn't kill you."

Zak paused and looked at Adam.

"Tell him you killed me then, to protect her." His voice cracked.

Adam nodded.

"I wish we could have had more time together," she whimpered as she fought back tears. "I should never have left you alone."

Zak squeezed her hand and smiled.

"You did what you had to. So did I."

Emma nodded and wiped a tear from her cheek.

Everything, from the woods around him to the words of her little brother, felt like a dream. Nothing seemed real anymore. Even the sound of her voice felt detached from herself. Maybe her mind was trying to calm her down and make her think this was a nightmare that she would soon wake up from.

"Please forgive me someday," he said in barely a whisper.

Suddenly, Emma was eight years old again. She grabbed her brother from the river as he thrashed wildly, trying to stay afloat. He'd been hopping along the rocks without a care in the world while Emma was fishing, jumping from one to the next until he'd missed his footing and fallen into the rushing water.

Emma dragged him to shore. His body was limp in her arms as she carried him onto the rocks. Time seemed to freeze as she pressed her hands firmly into his chest, trying to get him to breathe again. It felt like hours as she desperately tried to bring Zak back to life. Finally, he sputtered and coughed, spitting water out as he sat up.

The memory rushed away as quickly as it came, vanishing in an instant. Emma stared helplessly at her brother. This time, she wasn't eight years old and her brother hadn't been playing on the rocks. This time, she wouldn't be able to save him.

His hand fell lifelessly in her grip. His head slumped fully into the side of the chair.

His eyes were empty.

She had failed him.

He was dead.

Adam walked over to Emma and wrapped his arms tightly around her, pulling her into him as she sobbed. Her body heaved with each breath. Everything was spinning; her whole world had crashed down around her again. The one thing that mattered to her most – her baby brother – was gone.

"Emma," Adam said. "I'm so sorry."

He pulled her close and brushed his hand down her back as she cried. They sat on the forest floor outside Zak's cabin for several minutes while she sobbed.

"We'll take his body back to the Capital," Emma said in between breaths. "Then, I'll avenge him."

#

Charles ran his fingers through his hair. How was he going to clean up this mess? He'd dealt with a lot in his days of service, but today was undeniably the most stressful. His position of authority – his powers – everything were being put to the test. His mind raced as he thought of how he could best help Emma and Adam.

He would need to lead the troops by sea. Somehow he needed to convince the King that that was the best option. There was no time to waste.

The room reeked of smoke. The windows were open wide in an attempt to air out the room as medics ran around treating the injured men. Jason sat alongside his father, King Marcell, who rested in his throne and barked orders while a senior medic bandaged a gash on his arm.

"Charles!" The King yelled. "It's about time. Where were you?"

"I was down at the docks, sir," he replied. "I came as soon as I heard there was an attack. What happened?"

"Your damn pet came back, that's what happened," he retorted. Spit flew from his mouth, and his eyes darted around the room accusingly. "Look what she did!"

Charles looked around. He had to admit, the damage was impressive. The room looked like it had been under attack for hours, not just a few minutes. Tapestries lay smoldered on the ground, and scorch marks littered the walls. Several guards were still lying on the floor being treated for severe burns.

"I order you to take our best fifty men to kill Zak," the King said. "Bring the girl here alive. Everyone else can be killed."

"Yes, sir," Charles replied.

He looked at Jason. The prince's expression was blank and distant. Charles wondered if he realized what would happen to Emma and Adam if his father had his way.

"I'll take our fastest ship and head to Alsager immediately."

"No," the King thundered. "Go by land, you fool. It'll be faster, and I want her as soon as possible."

Charles shook his head and turned to Jason.

"Sir, with all due respect, I think we need to put up a defense using our troops on land," Charles said confidently. "I'd be surprised if the rebels don't launch an attack on the city when they hear what has happened. Going by sea would be better. That way, Prince Jason can lead a ground defense and protect us from the possibility of an impending attack."

Jason looked at Charles. If he knew what Charles was up to, he didn't show it. His stoic expression remained unchanged as he nodded.

"I agree," Jason said.

Charles thought of Elly.

He imagined her sitting in her room on the plush upholstered couch cradling the baby prince in her arms. She would be singing a soft lullaby coaxing him to sleep. Her voice reminded him of honey, smooth and rich. Jason's voice was similar to his mother's and Charles had long admired how similar Jason was to her. He was nothing like his father.

"As long as you bring me what I want, I don't give a damn what you do."

King Marcell looked away and barked more orders at the medics as he waved his hand dismissively at Charles.

#

Rays of sunlight filtered through the clouds as Charles walked to the docks. The King had already sent the orders ahead of him. Fifty of the best naval officers would be ready to disembark when he arrived. He would delay the boat as long as he could without arousing suspicion and hopefully that would buy him enough time to carry out the plan.

He paused as he stepped onto the wooden planks of the dock. In front of him was a small army of men boarding one of their fastest ships. Colonel Grant directed men onto the boat, his arms folded, his back straight and rigid.

"Hello, Charles!" he yelled, raising one arm high to greet him. "We're almost ready to disembark."

Charles walked forward, closing the distance between them. He looked at the ship.

"Have we made sure we have all the supplies we'll need?"

Colonel Grant nodded.

"We have everything packed and ready to go," he said. "Just waiting on a few men to return from the armory, and on you of course."

He laughed and patted Charles on the back.

"It's been too long, Charles," Colonel Grant said, a wide smile spread across his face. "I remember when we used to go on missions like this together. Back before you became Mr. Big Shot, working directly for the King."

"It has been too long, Grant," Charles replied.

He noticed the men returning from the armory out of the corner of his eyes. Time was up. There was no more stalling that could be done.

"I suppose we should get ready to head out."

"Of course!" Colonel Grant said as he motioned for the last few men to hurry up. They carried an armful of swords wrapped in a linen casing.

Charles sighed as he boarded the boat. Hopefully Emma and Adam had had enough time to carry out the plan.

CHAPTER 20

Charles exhaled heavily, his breath echoed in the stillness around him. Besides the occasional rustling of trees, it was complete silence. The morning light barely crept along the horizon in the distance, bringing with it a glow that bathed the edge of the forest. Charles' men stood at attention before him, quietly awaiting his orders.

Charles crossed his arms and stared at the trail ahead of them. Emma was out there somewhere, and he knew he had to lead the search to find her.

His heartbeat quickened as he turned back around to face his men. They looked back at him, expecting to be told to hunt down the girl. It's what the King would want after all, to see her punished. But that wasn't what Charles wanted. He needed to make sure she was safe. He owed her that much.

After another deep breath, he stepped back onto the hard wood of the dock and uncrossed his arms. He cleared his throat before he spoke.

"We'll head out this direction in search of Emma and Adam," he announced.

His gaze darted from one man to the next to meet everyone's eyes. His voice was loud and demanded authority.

"If you find them, you are to avoid harming them if at all possible. We'll want to keep them alive as prisoners. What they've done is unforgivable, and they have to pay for it."

A few of the men shared uneasy glances. They knew Emma, and they knew exactly what she was capable of. Emma could strike them down with ease if she wanted to, and leaving her uninjured greatly added to their own risk.

Suddenly, movement in the distance caught their attention. The sound of footsteps and hooves hitting the ground could be heard from where they stood.

Charles walked forward, stunned. Who could that possibly be?

The floorboards creaked under his weight as he moved. The sun glared over the trees directly at him now. His eyes adjusted to the light as he peered around.

Their facial features came into view, the silhouettes of their bodies illuminated against the light. It was Emma and Adam. They walked with their horse out of the woods; they seemed to be coming straight for the docks.

Charles sprinted up the trail towards them. The damp earth sunk slightly under each footstep as he raced. The thick, ankle-deep bushes slowed him down, but he wasn't stopping for anything until he found out what was going on.

Soon, Charles was close enough to see that Emma was limping, her body was held up mostly by Adam's arm around her waist. He ran his eyes over the horse and swallowed hard. A body rested lifelessly on it's back, a pale hand hung out from under an old blanket.

He couldn't believe it.

Her brother was dead

Memories of Emma as a little girl rushed to him. She had been so scared, so innocent, so selfless when he'd met her. All she'd longed for was a better life for Zak, ready to make whatever sacrifices that would take. Now, he was gone.

Charles cursed himself for having ever brought her to the Capital. If he hadn't, Emma would at least still have Zak – her only family – by her side. He blamed himself for reeling Emma in. He should have let her escape long ago. She didn't deserve any of this.

"Charles, we're glad you're here," Adam whispered. His voice, barely audible, was strained with exhaustion. "It's been a long day -- " He trailed off and glanced at the body out of the corner of his eye.

Emma looked up at Charles. She was pale, and her eyes were sunken and red. Charles had never seen her in such a state before. She looked weak; most of her weight leaned on Adam, who also looked like he was going to fall at any minute.

"I couldn't save him," she said softly, her eyes glued to the ground.

Charles raised an eyebrow at Adam as he reached forward to help support Emma.

"He had already poisoned himself when we arrived," Adam said as he handed Emma over to Charles. "He wanted his body brought to the King, in hopes that it would help end the fighting."

Charles nodded, trying to appear calm. The King would be furious. This was a foolish way for Zak to die, but that didn't matter right now. Besides, it was too late. His only concern now was getting them to safety and figuring out how to deal with King Marcell when they arrived back at the Capital. Even with the body, he would not forgive Emma for her earlier transgressions.

"Come with me," Charles said as he nudged Emma forward. She balanced herself unsteadily as they walked. "We'll get you in the boat and see what we can do."

As they approached the boat, the men stared silently. It was obvious from the way Charles held Emma around her waist that he did not see her as their prisoner, despite what he had said earlier. But no one dared to say anything as he led her into his quarters on the deck of the ship.

"Have the body placed into one of the wooden coffins from the hold. The King will want it when we make port," Charles instructed one of his officers as he led Emma and Adam inside.

The room was small, with only a few slivers of light peeking in through the narrow windows. An antique desk stood under a row of shelves across from a small single-person bed. Everything looked old and slightly tattered.

Charles sat Emma down on the edge of the bed and motioned for Adam to take a seat next to her.

"I won't allow the King to have your brother's body," Charles said firmly as he sat. "I have an idea."

He walked to the other side of the room and grabbed an old wooden trunk off the top shelf. It was covered in a thin layer of dust that Charles brushed off with his hand, sending specks of grey and black falling to the floor. The words "Field Kit" were carved into the top.

As he sat down next to Emma and Adam, he undid the clasps of the trunk and opened it, pulling out a small glass vial. It contained several thin strips of metal which looked silver in the light. The vial had a yellowed label with several indecipherable markings on it.

"What is it?" Emma asked. She took the vial from him and gently turned it in her hand as she inspected the metal strips.

"Magnesium. It's highly flammable, and once the fire is started it is almost impossible to put out. If we use this to burn your brother's body, they won't be able to stop it before he is turned to ash."

"Won't they be able to get water from the ocean to just put it out?" Adam asked.

"Magnesium will keep burning even after it is doused with water," Charles smiled as he grabbed two more vials out of the trunk. "Unless they have a lot of sand nearby, this will keep burning until it dies out on its own."

#

It took Charles several moments to process what had happened. He had seen death before, but never like this.

Suddenly, a hand reached out and grabbed his shoulder firmly. He spun around to face the man that stood beside him.

It was King Marcell.

To Charles' surprise, he looked tired and distant. Blood stained his face and jacket, and his hair was matted with dirt and sweat. His cheeks were sunken and his complexion pale. Charles couldn't remember a time when he'd seen Marcell look anything but regal, but today he was defeated and weary.

"Thank you for today, Charles," Marcell said in a low whisper, a stark contrast from his usual booming voice. "It was a hard day for us, and I appreciate you keeping up their spirits through all this --"

His voice trailed off as he looked around the battlefield, scanning the thousands of bodies that spread out in front of them.

"Bloodshed?" Charles asked.

Marcell nodded.

His hand, still perched on Charles' shoulder, shivered uncontrollably. Even through his thick wool jacket he could tell it was cold. Marcell had fought alongside his men, hoping he could inspire them to a quick victory.

Instead they'd had a battle that lasted two days, and took heavy casualties from both sides. Even though they had managed to take the stronghold, none of the survivors felt like victors. Only mourning and silence lingered over the fields of dead men.

They stood for several minutes in silence at the top of the wall, staring out over the land they had taken back from the enemy troops. It was a strategic victory. This fort was placed along the key trade routes to the Capital. With it under enemy control, many shipments of supplies had been intercepted in hopes of starving the people into rebellion.

Marcell had commanded a dual attack, one by land, the other by sea, to take back the fort. Charles had led the attack by sea and had taken out the enemy navy. By the time his men got into port, Marcell and General Johnson had made a full assault and broken through the gates. The plan worked.

General Johnson was one of the men that had been fatally wounded in the battle. He had served as Marcell's right hand man for almost ten years. He had been known for his steadfast loyalty and allegiance. His loss was a shocking blow to the war effort, and Charles could see the devastation on Marcell's face.

Tears lined Marcell's eyes as he stared into the distance.

"I'll need you to take Johnson's place as my advisor," Marcell said.

Charles nodded slowly as he contemplated the promotion.

He did not want to advise the King in times of war, as he knew from observing General Johnson how tough a task it would be. He could already foresee the sleepless nights, stressful days and endless planning ahead of him. But how could he refuse a man that had lost so much in this war already?

It had been five years since the Queen had been murdered, five long years since the start of the war. For years, this man had fought to defend his people from the invasion. He'd made tough choices, but so far they'd all been for the good of his citizens. Charles could not abandon him now.

It would not be long before the armies of Redholt sought revenge for this defeat. Charles worried that they would try to forge alliances, and that soon new enemies would be knocking at their door as well.

Footsteps echoed loudly behind them as someone walked up the steps to the top of the wall. It was Sergeant Lanston. He had just finished going through the troops and tallying up the casualties.

"How many injured, Lanston?" Marcell asked. "How many dead?"

Lanston grabbed a piece of parchment from his breast coat pocket and unfolded it.

"412 injured, 3214 dead, sir."

Marcell's jaw dropped. A tear escaped his eye and ran down his cheek.

"Thank you, Lanston," he said as he brushed the tear away. "Please make sure the injured are cared for, and burn the dead."

"Yes, sir." Lanston said.

He bowed and turned to return to the fort. It would take the rest of the evening to prepare the funeral pyres. It was a job that Charles wished upon no man, but one that he felt he should assist in.

"Sir," Charles said. "May I be excused to assist in cleaning the battlefield?"

Marcell stared at Charles blankly. His expression was dark and sullen, and his eyes were filled with regret. He nodded slightly and then turned to face out over the wall once more.

The work of piling bodies seemed endless. The row of corpses stretched out hundreds of feet in both directions, with logs scattered throughout to help kindle the flames and return them to the earth as ashes. Hours crawled by as he looked into the empty, lifeless faces of the young men as he dragged their remains to the pyre. These men would not live to see another day, say another word, admire another sunset. It could have so easily been Charles lying dead in the dirt instead of any of them.

A cold wind crept upon them as night approached. The sun offered them less warmth as they grabbed the last dozen bodies and added them to the pile. Torches were brought out from the fort to start the burning. The air reeked of blood and decay.

The sun began to set, splashes of amber and orange faded into the dark, overcast sky. Charles looked on in silence as the flames flickered in the air. The memory burned into his mind as he watched the skin of young men crackle and melt away as the pyres were eaten by the flames. Thousands of souls were sent into the evening sky, carried on the wisps of smoke, and each one took a piece of him with it.

#

The next morning, the boat brought them into Portishead. Within minutes of the ship docking, a dozen soldiers and the King stepped aboard. Prince Jason followed his father, trailing behind by a few feet as he stepped onto the deck of the boat. He avoided eye contact with Emma as he stood across from her, his arms crossed behind his back.

Emma and Adam's hands were balled into fists and bound tightly in a thick rope. Charles had insisted that they must look like prisoners when the King saw them; if not, the King might order something worse.

"It's about time you got back here with these traitors!" The King barked.

The anguish of the day before had clearly left him. He was back to his loud, usual self. He walked the length of the deck, stopping right in front of Charles and turning to face him.

"Where is the body?"

"Below deck in the hold, sir," Charles replied.

His posture was stiff and he looked the King directly in the eyes. He stood several inches taller than the King.

"My men are fetching it as we speak, sir."

The King nodded and walked back to stand beside Jason.

"Once we have proof that the rebel captain is dead, we can decide what to do with you two," he boomed.

Emma's heart raced as she felt a cool sweat form on her forehead. Part of her wanted to lash out and kill the King now. She could feel the blood rushing through his veins, pumping with each heartbeat. She knew she could easily make it stop, or reverse the flow if she wanted. He would convulse and collapse to the ground before dying slowly and painfully.

But she couldn't bring herself to do it, not with Jason there. Something about the way he looked, the way he stood, made her feel like he had a plan of his own. She couldn't accept that he'd willingly follow in his father's footsteps.

No. He must have a plan. I need to trust him.

Two men stepped onto the deck of the ship carrying a long wooden casket. The lid was detached, leaving the body plainly visible and exposed to the sea breeze.

Emma's stomach turned sour as she watched them place Zak's body on the deck. She hadn't seen him since they'd gotten to the ship, and now all the feelings of emptiness came rushing back to her. Her brother was gone, and this time, there was no chance of him coming back.

Numbness took over, slowly turning to exasperation and fury. She wanted to burn the ship to the ground with her and everyone else on it as revenge for what had happened.

As she contemplated ending everything, Adam leaned over slightly and pressed his shoulder into hers. His warmth was comforting. It reminded her that killing the King now wasn't the answer, that Zak would want her to carry on.

She watched in silent anger as the King hovered over Zak's body. He bent down and inspected it, as if he were observing an artifact. He poked at his lifeless limbs as he circled him like a hawk. A smile broke out from the corner of his mouth. He was clearly pleased with how things had turned out.

I've had enough.

Emma concentrated on the vials that Charles had placed alongside the body. She could sense the metal inside of them, their powers waiting to be unleashed. With as much precision as she could manage, she forced the metal to move against itself, creating a spark that would ignite the body.

A blinding white light cast over the deck as the magnesium ignited. Slowly but surely, small flares grew into thick, wild fire that quickly grew up alongside Zak's body and grabbed onto his clothes as they burned. The fire engulfed his entire body, spreading and eating away at his lifeless flesh.

"NO!" The King shrieked.

His ear-splitting scream resonated across the deck. His eyes widened as he watched the body burn to ashes.

In desperation, he pulled huge waves of seawater onto the deck, soaking the burning body and everyone that stood near it. The flames continued to burn, undeterred by the constant surges of water.

"NO, NO, NO!"

The King's anger rocked the entire boat as the sea beneath them surged. The deck flooded in several inches of water and everyone was drenched.

The body charred and blackened as the King continued to scream in outrage.

"Who did this?!"

He stomped towards Emma as best as he could in the ankle-deep water. His chest heaved up and down as he breathed heavily. His cheeks flushed from both the heat of the fire and his own anger.

"It was Captain Charles, sir."

A sheepish voice came from the side of the deck and everyone spun around. It was a young man, one of the newer men to the crew.

"I saw him place several vials alongside the body this morning before we docked. He must have planned it with these two traitors."

All eyes looked at Emma and Adam.

The King was silent for a moment. Then, he snapped his head towards Charles and barked, "You'll rot in a cell for betraying me. I always knew I shouldn't have trusted you as an advisor."

He swung his arm out and pointed a finger at them, spit spewing from his mouth as he continued to scream.

"Take them to the prison and lock them away. Let them starve while I decide what to do with them."

CHAPTER 21

A soft gray light filtered in through the barred windows as Emma awoke.

The prison cell was musty and damp, but not entirely uncomfortable. The bed was surprisingly soft, and the thick wool blanket had kept her warm all night despite it being a little chilly. Even so, she woke up several times from her stomach grumbling. It had been ages since she had eaten.

She rolled over onto her side to face Adam, who was still asleep on the bed across from her. He looked so peaceful as his chest gently lifted and fell with each breath, moving up and down at a calm, even pace. It suddenly struck Emma how brave he was for risking his life for her. Her stomach churned as she imagined how vulnerable they were now.

He turned his body to the right slightly, and pushed his whitish blonde hair out of his face as he moved. His hair was long now, almost to his chin, and he had a short beard as well. He'd changed so much since they'd first met.

He's so different now. Then again, so am I...

She was more muscular, fiercer and more intimidating than the girl she had been when she left Campton. Adam had told her a few days ago that the fire had been lit in her eyes, and now they glowed with a purpose that hadn't been there before. She knew that purpose was revenge.

She wouldn't quit until the King was stopped. She'd kill him if she got the chance.

"Emma," Charles whispered from across the room, startling her as she snapped out of her thoughts. "Are you awake?"

She propped herself up on the bed.

"Ye-yeah," she said with a yawn.

"Do you think you could break down this door if you need to?"

He sounded very articulate for someone who was still in bed. Emma guessed that he had been up for some time already, thinking about their options.

Emma looked at the door. There were bars of iron running vertically through it, intercepted by three thick pieces of oak – one close to the top of the door, one in the middle and one below. She focused on the door and felt the elements coursing through it and tested them by bending the iron and wood slightly.

The door creaked.

"Yes," she replied. "Are we going to try and escape?"

"Not unless we have a plan," he said. "Or unless we have to."

Emma didn't like the thought of breaking out. She knew that if they escaped, there was a chance of them being caught again. And if that happened, the King would not keep them as prisoners. He'd have them killed.

Adam began to stir awake and extended his arms out in a stretch.

He opened his eyes and turned to face Emma.

"We should come up with a plan, then," he said. He smiled sleepily. "I'm tired of being stuck in here."

Adam pushed aside his blanket and sat up on the side of the bed for a minute. Emma watched as he stood up and walked around the room. He was in just a pair of undershorts, and she could see the muscles in his legs tense as he walked. She admired him as he walked into the small bathroom that was attached to their cell and closed the door. He had become quite handsome over the past few years, and she wondered why she was only now realizing it.

Her mind wandered for a few moments before she brought herself back to what was most important. A plan. They had to figure something out, but Emma knew Charles would have issues with what she wanted to do.

She wanted to run back to the throne room and thrust a dagger in the King's heart. Every night since she'd watched Zak die, that's what had kept her going. She would get her revenge.

#

Jason stood with his arms folded loosely across his sides. It was risky for him to be down here. If his father caught him, he'd be locked up beside Emma and Charles. He knew it was worth the risk though, provided he could get them all to safety.

It was just before dawn and the guards in charge of the dungeon were changing shifts. They would only have a few minutes to make their escape. He hoped he'd have enough time to convince them.

Quietly, he waited near the side entrance of the dungeon for the two guards to walk up the stairs. They'd have to head back to the guardhouse in the opposite direction of where he stood, and he'd have about ten minutes to get down into the cells, unlock them, and convince Emma and Charles to leave with his mother and brother.

Almost time. Just another minute.

Two young guards marched out of the stairwell and made a turn at the corner of the stone wall, leaving the prisoners essentially unguarded. Jason knew it was time to make his move.

It was now or never.

Jason walked forward, moving as quickly as he could without making too much noise.

The gray stone of the stairs was slightly moist from the humidity of the prison, he had to be careful not to lose his footing. The last thing he needed was to trip and fall on his rescue mission. If he got caught, everything he'd planned over the past few days would be a waste. It was crucial that his father's reign passed smoothly to Jason. The future of his kingdom depended on it.

This dungeon was small compared to most, but it was the only one within the city. For most criminals, the King had them escorted outside of the capital and held in prisons that were tucked away in the rural country. He did this to make it more difficult for them to escape, but for certain prisoners he needed to keep them close as they posed a larger political threat.

It surprised Jason that this prison wasn't more heavily guarded, but he supposed Emma could break free of any prison, regardless of the security. If she wanted to.

The dungeon was quiet. Every footstep seemed to echo against the walls, no matter how quiet Jason tried to be. He decided that he might as well hurry since being stealthy wasn't working.

Within a few moments of briskly walking down the hall, he was at a large wooden door. This was where they were being held.

He reached his hand into his pocket and wrapped it around a key he had stolen earlier. He pulled it out, and pushed it firmly into the keyhole of the heavy iron lock. He gripped the key tightly and turned it.

The lock clicked.

He pressed his palm against the heavy door and gave it a push. It opened with a loud creaking noise.

A wave of cool, musty air washed over Jason as the door opened. He stood still in the entryway, shading his eyes from the sun that filtered in through the high window.

"Jason!" Emma gasped in disbelief. "What are you doing here?"

He looked around the room and noticed that Adam didn't seem happy at his arrival. He was frowning, his arms were crossed as he leaned against the wall.

"I've come to get you out," he replied.

"Emma could have broken us out, genius," Adam said harshly. There was a bite in his tone, a hardness they didn't often hear from Adam. "Do you have a plan for what to do after we're out?"

Jason nodded. He hadn't expected Adam to react this way, but he had it all planned out. He was positive he'd be able to convince them.

"You'll need to go to the merchant docks and steal a ship. It'll be the best way for you to escape the city undetected. My father has guards throughout the city, and they've all been told to keep an eye out for you. Most of his men are centered on the main streets, and the ones in charge of the seas are focused only around the main navy docks. He thinks that if you try to run, Charles will want a ship he's used to."

"That's true, I suppose." Charles laughed.

Jason smiled at him and said, "That's exactly what he thought too. That's why the three of you will take my mother and brother out of the Capital on a smaller ship. You'll be harder to detect that way —"

"Wait," Charles interrupted. "Elly is coming with us? The King will kill her if she's caught."

"That's why you have to make sure he doesn't get the chance," Jason said. His tone was deathly serious as he looked Charles in the eye. "I know how much she means to you. This is the best chance she'll ever have of escaping."

"But what about you?" Emma asked. She walked towards him. "What will you do?"

"I'll stay here and pretend to be loyal to my father," he replied. "The people will need me by the time this is all over."

"But it isn't safe for you here either," she said. "Let me stay and help you in secret. Charles can get the Queen and your brother out of the Capital and take them back to Redholt."

"You have to go," Jason said firmly. He placed a hand on her shoulder. "I need you to protect my family. Get them as far away from here as you can."

"Come with us then," Emma said. Her voice shook. "I'll take care of my business here and then we'll all run away together and start new lives."

Jason shook his head, trying to hide his frustration. If things were to go according to plan, everyone needed to follow along. They couldn't ask questions and suggest something else.

"My place is here. I have to make sure that when my father dies I take his place and make this country what it once was. I owe that to my people."

"I can't just leave you here with that monster!" Emma protested. "Let me kill him, and you can take his place now."

She has so much passion. Maybe I could go with her...

Impulsively, he leaned forward and kissed her.

His hand moved around behind her hip and pulled her in close, holding the kiss for several moments before finally breaking away.

Emma's eyes widened with surprise, her eyebrows arched at an angle. She looked at him in shock.

"You have to go," Jason said. "Please, trust me."

He pulled away and began walking down the corridor towards the stairs that led out of the prison. They couldn't wait any longer.

Emma lagged behind, stunned by what had just happened.

Jason wished he could go back and hold her in his arms and kiss her again and again, but he forced himself to keep walking forward. Getting his mother and brother out of the city needed to be his top priority, even if it meant losing Emma, even if it meant never seeing her again.

#

The morning light spread out over the city, casting long shadows in the streets. Most of the people were back in their homes still asleep. It was the perfect time to sneak out of the city and head to the merchant docks by the canal.

Elly met them at the entrance of the prison where Jason had instructed her to wait. She held her young son, Robert, in her arms. He was sleeping, wrapped snugly in a thin blanket. Emma hoped he would stay quiet as they fled. They'd be in for trouble if he suddenly started crying.

Jason quickly kissed his mother on the cheek and nodded to Charles that they were ready to leave. He glanced at Emma one last time before turning away. He left to distract the guards for their escape.

Charles stepped quickly in front of the group. He motioned for them to follow him as he edged around the corner and hurried down the alleyway. Their plan was to steal a small boat used for transporting fabric or spices between major cities. It would be strong enough to get them out of the country, but not large enough to be suspicious.

"Damn," Charles cursed under his breath, a scowl crossed his face and the skin around his eyes wrinkled in frustration. There were half a dozen guards pacing in front of the group, patrolling the only path they had to get to the boats. "We may have to fight our way to a boat after all."

Emma peered around the corner so she could see their opponents. They looked younger and less experienced than many others that she had dealt with on missions. The King must have assigned them here thinking that it was an unlikely route for them to use.

Emma had no doubt that she would be able to disarm them with minimal injuries. She motioned to Charles to lead Elly and Adam along the side of the street. They could wait there as she took out the guards.

Charles nodded and waved for the others to follow him. They crept around the corner into the shadows of the street.

It only took a few moments for them to disappear out of sight.

Emma waited until they were safely out of the way before sending a spinning burst of air towards the guards. She created a current that startled them and caused them to draw their swords.

She stepped calmly out of the shadows towards them.

All of the men dropped slightly into defensive positions, their swords pointed towards her. She could tell from their reactions that they had not expected a fight.

"Stop in the name of the King!" The tallest guard yelled.

His eyes locked onto hers as he took a step forward. His hand shook.

Emma waited until he was within a few feet of her before summoning a strong burst of air. Not seeing it coming, he fell flat against his back with a loud thump.

This is too easy. They aren't even elementalists.

With a quick swipe of her hand, Emma controlled another gust of wind and toppled all but one of the remaining guards over. The blow was powerful enough that it knocked them down hard. Their heads smacked hard against the ground. A few of them appeared to be unconscious, and the rest seemed unwilling to stand back up and fight.

As the last guard ran towards her, Emma focused on his sword and ripped it violently out of his hand before he could respond. She morphed the metal into a long, thick rod and used it to block the guard's path. The guard didn't react fast enough and it hit him sharply in his torso, causing him to exhale loudly and crumble to the ground.

Everything seemed to shake around them.

A strong pulse pushed the air in quick, hard motions, causing Emma to lose control of the metal. It fell to the ground with a loud, rattling clang. Everything looked like it was quivering slightly. A buzzing sound rang persistently in her ears.

She looked around her, staring at the fallen guards, trying to determine where the source of the pulse was coming from.

"You're not the only one that's been getting better, Emma!" A voice yelled, startling her.

John.

He stood in a bent-knee stance and wore a smirk on his face. His eyes burned with fury and determination. He sent out waves of energy in the air around him. It caused everything to feel distorted.

Harper walked out several feet behind him and watched silently as Emma tried to focus on the elements around them.

Nothing seemed to make sense; everything was moving in a way Emma had never felt before. She didn't feel like she was in control. The normal, predictable buzz of the world around her was spinning sporadically.

She desperately tried to focus on a piece of iron that was near John's feet. With all her energy, she concentrated on the iron and imagined it thrusting into him. Instead it just wobbled around limply, barely lifting off the ground.

John laughed.

"As long as I'm interfering with the air in just the right way, you'll never be able to keep track of what is moving and what isn't."

He turned away and continued to pulse the air around them. Emma felt dizzy and frustrated as she lost control of anything she focused on.

John continued to manipulate all his energy into the air, and Emma braced herself for an attack. Everything continued to vibrate.

Why isn't he attacking? I'm completely vulnerable.

"Now, Harper!" John called over his shoulder.

Suddenly it was obvious: He couldn't attack her while also vibrating the air.

Emma didn't know what was going to happen, but she braced herself. She noticed the hesitation on Harper's face.

"This isn't right John," she said slowly. There was a softness in her eyes as she spoke, a tone of understanding and sympathy.

"We can't do this to them. They're our friends."

"IT'S OUR DUTY!" He screamed.

His cheeks flushed. His eyes darted between Harper and Emma. He thrust his arm out and pointed at Emma.

"And she's no friend of mine!"

Harper frowned as she stepped forward to approach her partner. John seethed with rage, his body heaved up and down as he breathed. The contrast between the two of them was clear, and Emma wondered how they had ever worked together.

"We can't," she said as she placed a hand lightly on his shoulder. "I won't help you hurt them."

John scowled at her.

His face was red and sweat dripped down his forehead.

"You'd rather join these traitors? After all we've been through together?" He yelled at the top of his lungs. His voice was hoarse and filled with betrayal. A vein on his temple bulged. "It's because of that bitch, isn't it? She turned you against me."

"This isn't Emma's fault, John!" Harper screamed back at him while taking a step back. She took a deep breath and tried to compose herself. "You know that. You've just been jealous of her all these years and I'm done with it. I'm going with them."

John didn't move. His nostrils flared.

Suddenly, he jerked his hand upwards and sent a pulse of air towards her. Emma watched as Harper moved from side to side, skillfully dodging his attacks. She was able to weave and bob between them. She was too familiar with how he fought.

We don't have time for this.

Emma waited until John lunged forward again towards Harper. As he did, Emma focused on the iron that was lying next to him on the ground. She manipulated the bar and wrapped it tightly around his ankles. He toppled to the street with a loud thud, crashing face first to the ground.

CHAPTER 22

Harper leaned against the railing of the small wooden sailboat, and stared back at the dock. She pushed a long strand of blonde hair behind her ear and sighed. This might be the last time she saw Portishead, the only home she'd ever really had.

"Thank you for your help back there," Emma said. She stood a few feet behind Harper on the deck of the boat, next to several large burlap sacks of spices. "We wouldn't have made it without you."

Harper nodded, her face contorted as she tried to hold back tears. She had grown fond of John over the past few years, despite his many flaws. They'd been partners since they were brought to the capital, and she had been able to rely on him. She knew she had done the right thing, but she felt guilty for betraying him. She knew he'd be crushed that she'd left him.

"It was the right thing to do," she said as she stood upright and stepped back from the edge of the boat. "Let's just get out of here."

She walked to the bow of the boat and looked ahead of them. Charles helped the boat move between the rows of houses, gracefully pushing the water around the ship. They had left the sails closed for now, so that they could navigate the narrow paths that ran through the city and out to sea.

It was a beautiful sight, the earliest specks of daylight bounced off the rows of windows. The homes in this part of the city were all pressed up tightly against the water, and no space was left between them. It reminded Harper of a sea wall made of houses.

The stone wall that held up the homes cracked slightly, and some of the houses seemed to bow further in towards the canal than they should. Harper wondered if they would still be standing 100 years from now, or if they'd crumble into the water over time.

After several minutes of careful maneuvering through the canals, they came out onto one of the main channels. The passage would soon widen once they had turned the bend, and they'd be able to release the sails and make a run for the sea.

Harper noticed the walkways that lined the water were eerily vacant. Something felt wrong. People should be hurrying to get to the shops by now, and fishermen and merchants should be heading to their ships.

Harper blinked and tried to focus. They were almost to the mouth of the canal where they'd connect to the open sea. Everything they passed seemed to blend together. There were no people around. There hadn't been for several minutes.

"I think they may have locked down this part of the city," Harper said. "John must have warned them."

Charles looked around them and nodded.

"We're about to be ambushed," he said. "They'll try to cut us off before we get to open water."

Suddenly, the boat shook violently and flames ripped upwards.

Harper opened her mouth to scream, but nothing could be heard over the sound of the explosions around them. She flung her hands to her ears and desperately tried to close out the noise.

The boat rocked violently from side to side as a series of explosions cropped up around them. Several bags and crates caught on fire, and one of the sails was beginning to smoke.

Harper dashed towards the sail, desperately focusing on the water in the canal and bringing it up to put out the flames. She heard the loud thumping of footsteps as the guards made their approach from behind a few nearby buildings. There were at least a dozen guards flanking the port side of the boat.

They closed in on them.

Harper took a deep breath and focused on the fires. She watched as Emma launched small balls of spinning air at the guards, trying to push them back. There were so many of them that Emma seemed to be firing randomly, trying to split her attention between the guards and navigating the boat.

"We have to get out of here before reinforcements arrive!" Charles yelled over the sound of the fight.

Another series of explosions rocked the boat, knocking Harper to the deck. Her hands ached as she caught herself on the hardwood.

Where are those explosions coming from?

She surveyed the area as she braced herself on the railing.

A lone guard crouched behind a barrel on the other side of the canal. He only moved long enough to throw 2 small bombs at the boat before quickly hiding again. As the explosions rocked the ship, he moved further down the canal, keeping pace with them.

Harper pointed to the man on the other side as he ducked away again and yelled, "Emma, aim for that barrel!"

Emma turned around, confused. She couldn't see the guard, but sent a gust of air hurtling towards where Harper had pointed and knocked the guard several feet back.

Now Harper could focus on putting the fires out without more explosions. She pushed herself back up to her feet and began working on damage control while the others kept the guards at bay.

#

A tall guard in thick metal armor jumped down onto the deck of the boat. He let out a low growl as he landed.

He lunged at Emma, slamming his shoulder hard into her and knocking her back. She looked dazed as she tried to keep her balance.

Charles rushed forward and punched the guard hard in the jaw. Emma cringed at the sound of the bone cracking as the guard fell back into the railing. More guards rushed down towards the boat, and two more jumped down onto the deck.

Adam rushed the guard nearest to him, trying to pull water up from around the boat to slow him down while Charles and Emma dealt with the others. Harper worked desperately to try and keep the flames from spreading.

We need to get out of here. Now.

Adam looked over just as Charles was struck with a sharp piece of metal across the side of his head. It had been thrown by one of the guards that still stood on the low wall next to the ship. The guard smirked as he pulled back his hand to throw again.

Charles wiped his mouth with the back of his hand, smearing blood across his lips. His expression changed as he frowned at the guard. He looked angrier than Adam had ever seen him. His pale blue eyes had a fire in them as he ran towards the edge of the boat, pushing himself up on the railing with a strong jump, leaping up to where the remaining guards stood.

Elizabeth shrieked and grabbed a dagger from her waist. She threw it at the nearest guard without pausing to aim.

"No! You can't have him!" She screamed as she ran towards the side of the boat.

The dagger lodged itself deep into the guard's bicep. He spun his attention towards the boat and scowled.

"Stop!" Adam yelled. He rushed towards Elizabeth as she struggled to climb onto the railing of the ship nearest the dock.

Adam grabbed her by the shoulders and firmly tugged her back into the boat. She flailed onto the deck on her back.

The guard that she had struck jumped down into the boat beside Adam. He punched Adam as he leapt down.

The blow made his head spin, and his stomach felt sour. Everything seemed blurry as he lashed out at the guard.

Harper ran into the side of the guard's body and pushed him hard against the ship's railing. He struggled to regain his balance and grabbed onto Harper's coat to try and pull himself up. She pushed back at him.

Harper struggled to keep the guards hands away from her throat. He was much stronger than she was.

Adam laid motionless on the deck as the two struggled above him. Then as Harper pushed hard against the guard, he managed to move his leg out beneath the guard to trip him. It was just enough to give Harper the edge, and with a firm shove she was able to knock him over the railing.

The guard screamed as he fell between the boat and the canal wall into the water, his sounds were muffled as the water overtook him.

They were almost to the edge of the canals now, and within a few seconds they'd be in open water and able to release the sails for their getaway.

Just a little more.

Adam jumped to his feet, his head spinning. The guards were distracted by Charles, now was their chance.

Every muscle in Adam's body tensed as he focused his energy on the water around them. His mouth dried, and tears sprung to his eyes as he pushed them quickly away from the guards and away from Charles into the open sea.

"No!" Elizabeth screamed, sobbing. "We have to go back. We can't leave him."

"We can't go back," Emma said as she helped Adam move them swiftly out into the open waters. They needed to get further away, it's what Charles would have wanted.

#

It felt like ages since they'd made it to sea and lost sight of the capital behind them.

Everything felt so different now.

Emma stepped out of the small cabin and onto the deck of the ship where everyone waited for her. The sea lapped against the boat as they ebbed back and forth. She felt like she was going to vomit as she thought about how Charles had sacrificed himself. They had made it to sea and were free now, but he would be killed if he had survived that ambush. It almost didn't seem worth it now, knowing that he and Zak were both gone.

She steadied herself on the railing and walked forward, forcing herself to focus. All of her friends looked at her, hoping she'd know what to do next. She felt just as lost as they did, but she had a plan.

"What do we do now?" Adam asked.

Everyone's eyes rested on Emma, waiting while she pondered the question. She wiped the sleeplessness away from her eyes.

"We're going to get help," Emma said finally.

She looked down at her feet and sighed.

"We're almost to Ban Lian. We're going to meet the Emperor and ask for his help to bring down King Terril."

"Do you really think he'll help?" Harper asked.

The Emperor shut down the city of Ban Lian years ago after building a wall around it to shut out the terrors of the war.

"He hasn't been heard from since the wall was built. The city went completely silent."

"Not completely silent," Elizabeth said quietly. "They've maintained communication with Redholt in secret."

Harper scratched the back of her head and raised an eyebrow, "But why would they do that? They've gone completely dark to the rest of the world."

"My people have never truly given up on the war, and neither has the Emperor," Elizabeth paused and looked out over the water behind them. "I've never told anyone this, but I was married off to keep an eye on the King, not to bring peace between our kingdoms."

She looked down at her feet. Her hands clasped tightly in front of her hips.

"I fell in love with the people of Durisdeer," she said. "I never wanted war to rip our kingdoms apart again, so I lied in my reports. I betrayed my home to try and keep the peace."

Everyone stood silently for several moments. They were all in disbelief at how many years Elizabeth had suffered as Queen for this secret.

"I know now that war is inevitable," she said as she looked up at Emma. "The king has to be stopped at any cost. What he's doing to the refugees is just horrible. I can't stand by and watch it any longer."

Tears came to the corners of her eyes, her long eyelashes flickered quickly to bat them away. Starting the war would mean countless casualties on all sides, and they'd have no guarantee of defeating King Terril's armies.

"Then that's what we'll do," Emma said. "We'll convince the Emperor to go to war and take Durisdeer by force."

She turned away from them and walked in silence to the helm of the boat. Her heart ached as she saw the giant walls of Ban Lian stretch out along the horizon. The shoreline was shrouded in a thick dark fog that seemed to devour all the light that entered.

There was no going back now. Her brother and Charles were gone, and she had no home left. All she could do now was fight so that they hadn't died in vain.

As they approached land, the sun faded below the horizon and a bitter wind rushed over the ship. It pushed at Emma and Adam as they steered the boat to shore.

Adam reached out slowly and grabbed Emma's hand in his. He held it tightly as they let themselves get swallowed up by the darkness that covered the shores of Deoria.

Made in the USA
Coppell, TX
18 February 2021